"I am here to ask you to become my wife."

Selena laughed. "You're not serious."

"I assure you, I am very serious," Nicholas said.

"But why would you ask such a thing? You don't love me."

His expression grew hard. "Love doesn't enter into this at all."

The smile faded from her face. "I don't quite understand."

"I also find myself at somewhat of a loss," he said. "You know, Selena, this is the first time I've ever proposed."

"But you've been married," she protested, then her eyes narrowed. "Oh. That was an arranged marriage, wasn't it?"

"Yes, my first marriage was arranged," he said calmly.

"I see. Well, no matter. I appreciate your offer of marriage, but the answer is no."

"Is there someone else?" He spoke quickly, irritated by her instant refusal.

"No," she answered, just as quickly. "I simply don't wish to be married."

Dear Reader,

It's February—the month of love! And what better way to celebrate St. Valentine's Day than with Silhouette Romance.

Silhouette Romance novels always reflect the magic of love in compelling stories that will make you laugh and cry and move you time and time again. This month is no exception. Our heroines find happiness with the heroes of their dreams—from the boy next door to the handsome, mysterious stranger. We guarantee their heartwarming stories of love will delight you.

February continues our WRITTEN IN THE STARS series. Each month in 1992, we're proud to present a book that focuses on the hero and his astrological sign. This month we're featuring the adventurous Aquarius man in the enchanting *The Kat's Meow* by Lydia Lee.

In the months to come, watch for Silhouette Romance books by your all-time favorites such as Diana Palmer, Suzanne Carey, Annette Broadrick, Brittany Young and many, many more. The Silhouette Romance authors and editors love to hear from readers, and we'd love to hear from *you*.

Happy Valentine's Day... and happy reading!

Valerie Susan Hayward
Senior Editor

MARION SMITH COLLINS

Every Night at Eight

Silhouette Romance

Published by Silhouette Books New York

America's Publisher of Contemporary Romance

To Tara Hughes Gavin.

SILHOUETTE BOOKS
300 E. 42nd St., New York, N.Y. 10017

EVERY NIGHT AT EIGHT

ISBN: 0-373-08849-3

First Silhouette Books printing February 1992

Books by Marion Smith Collins

Silhouette Romance

Home To Stay #773
Every Night at Eight #849

Silhouette Intimate Moments

Another Chance #179
Better Than Ever #252
Catch of the Day #320
Shared Ground #383

MARION SMITH COLLINS

has written nonfiction for years and is the author of several contemporary romances, as well as one book of general fiction.

She's a devoted traveler and has been to places as far-flung as Rome and Tahiti. Her favorite country for exploring, however, is the United States because, she says, it has everything.

In addition, she is a wife and the mother of two children. She has been a public-relations director, and her love of art inspired her to run a combination gallery and restaurant for several years.

She lives in Georgia with her husband of thirty years.

BULGARIA

Black Sea

GREECE

TURKEY

KARASTONIA

Aegean Sea

N

TURKEY

All underlined places are fictitious.

Chapter One

Nicholas Saber looked out the cabin window. The definition of the runway was blurred not only by the aircraft's speed but also by a heavy rain. The nose of the sleek private jet lifted and Nicholas felt the aerodynamic pressure push him gently against the back of his seat. Suddenly, as though plucked by a celestial string, the plane climbed quickly into the air, past the clouds, into the blue afternoon sky above Boston's Logan Airport and leveled off.

Saber unfastened his scat belt and rose to his feet. He stretched his long arms over his head. His fingers brushed the ceiling. He had changed from comfortable traveling clothes, in which he had crossed the Atlantic, to a dark suit, white shirt and tie. The journey was almost over. This was the last leg, this comparatively short hop from Boston to Washington, D.C.

"I'll be damned grateful to get out of this airplane," he said to his companions, a man and woman who were the only other passengers.

A white-jacketed steward appeared at the curtain that divided the cabin from a forward compartment. "Would you like hors d'oeuvres or drinks, sir?" he asked.

Saber indicated his guests. "Bree? Ryan? What will you have?"

"I'd love some coffee, thanks," Bree O'Hara answered. Lovely, dark-haired Bree wore a simple silk dress in bright crimson, her best color.

"I might like—" began her husband, Ryan.

"Black coffee," Bree finished for him. "Watching our weight, remember?" She smiled sweetly at her husband's frowning face.

Ryan O'Hara was the police commissioner for the city of Boston. When Saber had first met the couple nearly two years ago, Ryan had just been appointed to the position and was responsible for security during Saber's visit to the United States in his official capacity as Karastonia's foreign minister. They had remained good friends.

The police commissioner had been determined to continue active participation. But he'd since learned the bane of administrators everywhere—all paperwork and no action. Blend that with marriage—a contented, happy marriage, as he'd told Nicholas— and fatherhood, and before he knew it Ryan had gained fifteen pounds.

Saber watched them carefully, a small cynical smile on his lips. When love was involved, marriage became a crapshoot, a roll of the dice. But his friends seemed to be making it work. Maybe they were the exception that proves the rule.

True to Saber's expectation, Ryan couldn't maintain a grumbling facade under the force of that sweet smile. "Damn desk job," he growled good-naturedly.

Nicholas laughed. He'd already heard this complaint. "Coffee for all of us," he told the steward.

The steward returned with a tray and set it down on the table between the seats. When they'd been served, the man disappeared again into the forward compartment.

"Now, Saber, do you want to tell us what this is all about?" asked Bree. "Not that we aren't delighted to spend a weekend in such distinguished company—"

Saber snorted. "Bree, you of all people?" Then he smiled. In the presence of his friends he was beginning to relax.

Bree kept a straight face. "I was referring to your position as distinguished Godfather to one April Nichole O'Hara. Is there something else you do?" she asked with mock innocence.

Saber laughed. "That's right. Put me in my place," he quipped. But, as usual, any mention of the adorable six-month-old tyrant who ruled the O'Hara roost provoked a reflective, melancholy feeling within him. "I'm getting married," he announced without further preamble.

"Who is she? Do we know her?" Bree and Ryan both spoke at once. They had visited Karastonia on several occasions, including Saber's inauguration as the first elected president of the country, and had met a number of people, so Bree's question came as no surprise. She was clearly delighted at the idea. "Was she at the inauguration?"

"No, she was unable to be there," said Saber brusquely, remembering the inauguration festivities with a feeling akin to aversion. In fact, during that hectic week he had begun to formulate the plan to remarry. He'd had it brought home to him just how much he needed a hostess, a companion, a wife, at his side.

The king of Karastonia, who had no direct heir, had decided two years ago to set aside the monarchy in favor of democracy. Foreign Minister Saber was the king's cousin and could conceivably have made a case for ascension but he had absolutely no ambition in that direction.

Besides, he agreed wholeheartedly with the king, who felt the time had come to join the worldwide march toward government by the people. He had not agreed with the king, however, that all the plans could be implemented and elections held within one year. But as long as his cousin ruled, he was bound to obey.

It had been a heady and exhausting experience, playing midwife at the birth of a brand-new democracy. And it had not been an easy delivery. Though most of the dissident voices were now grumbling their acceptance, there were still people who thought Karastonia should continue under the centuries-old monarchy.

When the elections were held—at the end of the prescribed year—the majority of his countrymen felt that Saber was the logical choice for president. Admittedly, he had the experience, the dedication and the love for his country. But now, after one year in office, he was beginning to wonder about his endurance.

He was tired. And he was lonely. And so he would take a wife. "You probably don't know her, but you'll meet her this weekend. She's from Virginia," he answered Bree's first question at last.

"She's an American?" asked Ryan, his brows lifting in surprise.

"Her mother is. She has dual citizenship. She's the daughter of our hosts this weekend. Her name is Selena Mastron."

Selena Cybele Victoria Mastron's image rose in his mind as smoothly and as effortlessly as his breath filled his lungs. She was pretty enough, though not a beauty as he remembered her. But she had other, more valuable qualities. Statuesque, dignified, she was extraordinarily intelligent, had natural poise and warmth, a sense of humor and—he added to himself with a slight quirk of his mouth—a good body. Her smoky gray eyes held a hint of sensuality without being unseemingly seductive.

Selena's calm, perceptive intelligence and traditionalism were contributions from her father, retired Karastonian ambassador to the United States. Her grace, as well as her freewheeling independence—the only characteristic that gave him pause—were inherited from her American mother, a former prima ballerina.

Saber had considered long and carefully before coming to the conclusion that Selena would be a perfect wife for him despite her occasional tendency to be a bit too forthright and outspoken. The job he needed her to fill required her cosmopolitan attitude, her dignity, her enterprise, her vitality.

And, at thirty-four, she was mature enough not to expect a vow of eternal love—which was the one thing he couldn't offer.

He described her to his friends, then he went on to explain, "Her father is Karastonian but she was born here and grew up here." He hesitated. "There's one small obstacle," he added soberly. "Selena doesn't know that her father and I have arranged this marriage."

His words were greeted by a long silence. He noted that Bree set her cup down with great care; Ryan's jaw had gone slack.

"An arranged marriage?" murmured Bree, disconcerted. "I didn't know that sort of thing still went on." She cleared her throat and gave a little laugh. "She sounds extremely...appealing but, Saber, you may be in for trouble."

He smiled at their uneasy exchange of glances. "That's why I especially wanted you two to fly down to Virginia with me for the weekend. I know that American women are different, and I want your advice as to the best way to handle it."

Selena pulled into the four-car garage between her mother's Lincoln and her father's Range Rover. The other vehicle was a sporty runabout model. Her car looked like a poor relation in comparison. *Poor old Pinto,* she thought to herself, as she switched off the engine. As long as a vehicle worked properly and got her where she wanted to go with a minimum of fuss, she didn't particularly care what kind it was.

She sighed, got out of the car and stepped from the building into the last rays of fading sunlight. She shivered; though spring had officially arrived three weeks ago and new blooms seemed to pop out daily, a slight chill remained in the air. She took her small suitcase out of the back.

The sight of her family home, as always, warmed and soothed her. She smiled. Located in suburban Virginia outside Washington, D.C., the two-story manor-style house was an island of peace and quiet set amid rolling lawns and shaped boxwood, formal gardens and bridle paths. The pebbled walkway crunched under her sneaker-clad feet as she headed toward the house; she inhaled the fresh, sweet scent of the early jasmine vine that shaded the trellis near the side door.

Spring break. To her students it meant a trip to the beach; to Selena it meant going home. She could look forward to being pampered for a few days. She smiled, too, at the memory of her adolescent resentment and rebellion toward the attention and coddling she received as an only child.

But no more. She wouldn't resent the coddling this week. This week she was going to revel in it. Her steps quickened in anticipation.

Thank heavens the long, tedious interval of professional pressure at the college where she taught was over. No more interviews, conferences, discussions, no more scrutiny of her private life to judge whether she was worthy, in the eyes of the college administration, of tenure. All the questions had been asked; all the testimony given. Now she simply had to await the verdict.

There was competition, of course, and she would have to live with the uncertainty for a few more hours. A friend of hers, Van Styles, was also under consideration. She liked Van; at one time she'd thought he might have become more than merely a friend. But she had been with the college nearly two years longer, and, to be honest, she was a better teacher. That was one of the reasons the relationship hadn't worked out.

The decision of tenure was taken very seriously indeed by the committee that recommended candidates to the board of governors of the college. After tenure was offered and accepted, the board expected the tenuree to remain with the school until he or she died or retired, whichever came first. The committee weeded out the persons who might not be fully appreciative of that singular honor, and once they made their recommendation, the matter was as good as settled. The committee, however, had been unable to arrive at a decision.

This morning she'd been informed of yet another delay. This latest holdup didn't bode well for her cause, she knew, and she was angry over it. But she managed to control her impatience.

The side door leading to her mother's morning room was locked. Odd. Selena rattled the knob, shrugged and headed around to the front entrance.

Though the members of the committee hadn't come right out and admitted so, this latest delay in the promotion process was prompted by the fact that she was an unmarried woman. The subject of her marital status had first arisen earlier this week. The men wanted guarantees that she was not planning marriage. The question was such a surprise, that she'd hesitated.

They had not been pleased at her hesitation. Their prissy little comments about things like biological clocks and maternal instincts had been almost comical. She'd recovered quickly, reassuring them that she had no plans at present for marriage or a family.

But the damage had been done. She could tell by their frowns and thin-lipped silence. She'd had to remind them, subtly, of course, that such questions on their part were illegal as hell.

She climbed the shallow steps, crossed the broad veranda and tried the front door. It was locked, too. Perplexed, she pushed the bell, and pushed it again.

The man who opened the door was an unsmiling stranger in a three-piece suit. His demeanor and his thorough scrutiny screamed security.

Selena was not unfamiliar with the type. "Ah-h-h, hello," she said, more puzzled than alarmed. Having grown up in a home where a person of any nationality was apt to turn up at any time, entourage in tow, she wasn't particularly surprised.

"You're Ms. Mastron?" demanded the man sharply.

No accent. That was interesting. His dour face was inscrutable. He was not extremely tall but his broad shoulders almost filled the doorway. He examined her very carefully, as though she were a specimen with which he was unfamiliar. That could very well be. She wasn't exactly dressed for visitors. Her faded blue denim slacks were casual and worn enough to be comfortable, and her blue shirt was rumpled. The pretty pink sweater vest, knitted by her mother, was the only decent-looking item of clothing she wore.

By the time he had concluded his appraisal of her, she had the feeling of having been dissected, examined and laid out to dry. "Dr. Mastron, actually," she said, wondering if she had proclaimed her title in an effort to establish some degree of credibility with this person. If so, it hadn't worked.

"Won't you come in?" he said woodenly.

Before she could recover from the amazement of being politely invited into her parents' house by a total stranger, and a mean-looking one at that, her mother emerged from the drawing room.

"Darling, I thought I heard the bell. I'm so glad you're here."

"Mother, is anything wrong?"

Selena was enclosed in a warm, fragrant hug. "Nothing, dear," said Jayne Mastron, a hint of laughter in her eyes as she drew back and looked at her daughter. She frowned, but it wasn't because of the clothes. Jayne was accustomed to her daughter's traveling wardrobe. "You look tired."

Before she could assure her mother that she was indeed very tired, Jayne took her under her arm and waved her free hand toward the stranger.

"And this is Mr. Smith."

Sure he is, thought Selena. And I'm Minnie Mouse. She nodded her acknowledgment of the introduction. "Mr. Smith."

"Saber is going to visit us over the weekend," Jayne went on to explain. "He should be arriving within the hour."

Selena did not like the little skip of anticipation that her heart delivered at the news of Nicholas Saber's imminent arrival. She reminded herself that she'd recovered from her adolescent fascination with the handsome widower long, long ago.

Nicholas Saber was the president of Karastonia, the tiny, beautiful country on the Aegean Sea that was her father's homeland. She looked around to discover that Mr. Smith—she'd been correct about his security status—had melted away.

With a philosophical shrug Selena laid aside her expectations for a relaxing holiday. She certainly wouldn't be pampered, not with Saber around. She wouldn't be able to throw on another old pair of jeans and ride wild over the countryside whenever she felt like it. She wouldn't be able to pour out her frustrations over her job to her mother—who would understand—and her father who wouldn't understand, but who would comfort her, anyway.

On the other hand, things seemed to . . . happen . . . whenever Saber appeared. He had a knack for bringing excitement in the room with him, as though he donned it with his clothing. And wherever he went, whether he sought the attention or not, he became the focal point of any gathering.

"Saber's friends from Boston, the O'Haras, are coming, as well. Do you remember us mentioning that we met them at the inauguration?"

She caught her breath. "Yes," she said softly. But the name O'Hara brought forth an uglier, more vivid memory. "Isn't he the police commissioner who helped save Saber's life when he was in Boston several years ago?"

Jayne chuckled but her eyes were serious as she laid her hand on her daughter's chilled cheek. "To hear Ryan tell it, Saber didn't need his help." She glanced at her watch. "You have plenty of time to change later, Selena. Leave your bag, and come into your father's study for a few minutes. We have a fire in there. I hope it's the last one of the season."

Selena dropped her bag at the foot of the stairs and followed her mother down the hall. "Where is Daddy?"

"He's—"

"Right here, my darling," said a voice from behind them.

Selena turned to be immediately warmed by her father's smile. He'd just come in from outside and his hair was windblown. She noted that he was moving stiffly as though he'd pulled a muscle. He'd probably been riding his rascally old stallion, Black Snow.

"Hi, Daddy." Again she was enveloped in a hug, this one secure and enthusiastic and smelling of rich pipe tobacco. She hugged him back, her enthusiasm equal to his; she adored him.

But when she drew away to look more closely at his face she noticed a pale cast to his skin that hadn't been there the last time she was home. She was probably imagining things. She schooled her features into familiarity and affection. "How are you?"

"I'm fine," he said heartily—too heartily.

Turnus Mastron was not quite as tall as his wife or daughter but he managed to take both of them under his arms and together they entered the room where a fire blazed merrily on the hearth. "Your mother told you that Nicholas is coming for the weekend?" There was a hint of pride in his voice. His close friendship with the charismatic leader was a point of pride to him.

Selena tried to reclaim some of her earlier animation as she held out her hands toward the fireplace. "Yes, she did. I am properly impressed, I assure you. Is this an official visit?"

"Not this weekend, no. He will spend the better part of next week in Washington attending to state affairs but he has some personal business to attend to first," he answered with a satisfied expression.

Jayne shot her husband a speaking look.

"A vacation weekend," he amended, trying to disguise the pleasure in his accomplishment. He went to a serving cart that held the makings for drinks and began to prepare a Scotch for himself and two small, stemmed glasses of dry sherry for Selena and her mother.

Selena had intercepted the look that passed between her parents but she chose to ignore it. Most likely there was some minor crisis that Saber wanted her father to advise him on and her mother was cautioning discretion. Though Turnus had retired as Karastonia's ambassador to the United States, he was often called upon for consultation. Her mother said it kept him young.

She turned her back to the fire, took the glass her father offered and sipped tentatively. The liqueur was really too heavy for her taste but her father thought all women should drink sherry and all men, Scotch. She'd long ago given up arguing with him.

"Well, Selena, are you going to keep us in suspense?" asked Jayne, leaning forward from her seat on the sofa. "Did you get your promotion?"

Selena sighed and set her glass aside as she joined her mother on the sofa. "I still don't know. Now the committee says they'll announce their decision this week."

"But that's what they said last week," protested Jayne.

Selena nodded. "And the week before that. They've raised a new question now," she said, unable to keep the irony from her voice. "I'm afraid the old maids are worried that I might be hit by the nesting urge."

"The old maids?" said Turnus, clearly puzzled. "I thought the committee was made up of men."

Her father had lived in this country for thirty-five years and he rarely had trouble with idioms, but Selena smiled and explained, "They *are* men, Daddy, but they are old maids in any case. To translate—they're wondering if I will want to marry and have a family." She shrugged. "I tried to tell them that the thought never entered my mind, but they don't want to hand out tenure to a woman, anyway. And to convey the honor and have her resign in favor of a husband and a baby would be a disaster."

"I can understand that," said Turnus thoughtfully.

"Daddy." She shook her head in resigned amusement and looked at her mother, who seemed to be choking on something. "I don't know how you put up with him," she added, laughing. "I suppose I'd better change my clothes before the distinguished guests descend upon us." She rose and crossed to her father's side and kissed him on the cheek. "You old chauvinist," she said fondly.

It was an accusation that had been made many times in this house when she was young, she recalled as she climbed the stairs to her room. But the amusement had long since replaced her adolescent rancor. She still had trouble comprehending her mother's acceptance of the old-world, male domination that seemed inbred in Turnus.

But Selena had her own life now; her father's chauvinistic standards didn't affect her any longer, thank goodness.

The dining room had grown relatively quiet as the people around the polished mahogany table addressed their food. The civilized clink of silverware on china, and the soft muffled footsteps of the butler as he served, removed, and kept the wineglasses filled, were the dominant sounds. The occasional murmur was almost a surprise accent to the hushed atmosphere.

Something was up, thought Selena, as she chewed thoughtfully. Her gaze traveled from one of her dinner companions to the next; she seemed to be the only one who wasn't knowledgeable. From the moment they'd gathered together, she'd sensed a watchfulness, a cautious expectation emanating from the other five. The aura of expectation was so strong that it sang in the air and seemed to envelop the whole house.

She would have been worried about a world crisis of some kind, if the others weren't all so—so—*jolly* was the only word she could come up with to describe their behavior, but it wasn't really a good description.

Even her father seemed in excellent spirits, and she was convinced now that he was not feeling well. Over a succulent bite of quail, smothered Southern-style, her eyes met those of Bree O'Hara. She smiled with her eyes.

The smile was returned, but the pretty brunette was as edgy as everyone else and—Selena didn't like this observation—she thought she saw sympathy in Bree's eyes.

Ryan interjected with a remark about the food and the visual contact was broken before she could really judge it. She set aside the disquietude prompted by that look, deciding she must have misread it.

She had avoided looking at Saber, seated to her left. But he'd had no such reservation. In fact his eyes had widened in surprise when he'd greeted her. Now she felt his gaze resting often on her profile.

She was dramatically aware of him. Warmth seemed to emanate from his large frame, his deep voice sent shivers through her, and the fresh, clean smell of his distinctive after-shave drifted toward her. She began to wish she had worn something more conservative than the rose silk that left her shoulders bare.

She hadn't seen him in over a year but he was as handsome as she'd remembered. No, he was more so. Maturity enhanced his looks as well as his self-confidence. Though the silver strands in his hair were more numerous now than the last time she'd seen him, the gray was insignificant in his thick hair. He was still physically powerful, as well. Strength radiated from him. And his dark eyes still held a hint of sensuality and, surprisingly, laughter, even beneath the burden of arduous responsibility that was reflected there.

On her right, at the head of the table sat her father, another disturbance. He had barely touched his dinner. She was beginning to worry seriously about his health.

"Selena?" Her mother's voice interrupted her thoughts.

Selena resented the rush of color that stained her cheeks. "I'm sorry, Mother. Please forgive me for being such an automaton tonight," she added to the others around the table.

Bree came to her rescue. "I understand you are waiting for news of a promotion?"

Now, how in the world had Bree O'Hara known that? "Yes. The dean of the history department retired unexpectedly last year, leaving some gaps in the faculty. I'm hoping for tenure." She couldn't explain further without going into all her frustrations, and such complaints were hardly acceptable for dinnertable conversation. She waved her hand dismissively. "The politics of academia are sometimes hard to explain."

"As are politics in general," inserted Saber smoothly. He went on to tell an amusing anecdote about a French representative to the United Nations, known to be a rather snobbish gourmet, being stranded in a small southern town in the United States and being forced to breakfast in a café called Mom's. Saber swore that the man was now trying to corner the export market on grits.

The others laughed and Selena sent him a grateful glance.

"Would you like something else, Nicholas? More wine?" asked Jayne when they'd finished with dessert.

"No, thank you, Jayne," Saber answered, distracted once more by a movement from Selena next to him. He'd noticed the fatigue that touched her lovely face—that face that had been such a shock to him—and wondered what had caused it. He hoped to hell she wasn't troubled over a love affair. That could complicate things. He was unaware of the frown that chased across his brow.

"Then, shall we have our coffee in the living room?" Jayne rose.

Saber got to his feet and held the chair for Selena. She threw a polite, if absent, smile of thanks over her shoulder and preceded him out of the room. Just before they reached the door to the living room he stopped her with a touch at her elbow. "I need to talk to you alone for a few minutes." He leaned forward and spoke in a low voice so the others wouldn't overhear. He realized suddenly that his lips were only inches from her bare shoulder. The skin there was unblemished, as smooth as creamy satin. He straightened abruptly to meet her blank expression.

"Now?" she asked as she turned. She had spoken too sharply, drawing the stares of the others.

He frowned and ignored the sudden silence and varying looks from the other four people. Turnus's smile was confident; Jayne's was anxious; Bree and Ryan still wore traces of the initially stunned, then dubious, expressions with which they had greeted his announcement on the plane this afternoon.

He'd dismissed the warnings of his friends that convincing Selena to marry him would be a difficult task. Not that he'd ever really believed it would be easy, but he knew his own powers of persuasion and he was confident that Selena would agree to be his wife. He regretted the need for haste but the obvious fact that she was disturbed about her job might be a plus. "If this is a convenient time for you," he said formally.

Selena's tired look turned into one of concern as she saw him frown and she realized that she had become the focus of attention. "Well, no. I mean I don't mind. Would you like to talk in Father's study?"

Saber nodded. Aware of the sudden uneasiness that chased across her features, he gave her a reassuring smile. "Thank you." He glanced at Jayne. "Will you excuse us?"

"Certainly," she answered quickly. "Shall I have coffee sent to you?"

Saber hesitated. "No, we'll join you shortly."

Jayne nodded and led the others into the living room while Saber followed Selena down the hall and into the study.

Chapter Two

As he entered the study behind Selena, Saber's mind registered several things, the first of which was her unforeseen and unexpected sensual appeal. He'd always known she was attractive but this beautiful, sexy woman was not the one he'd remembered when he'd made his plans.

Her hair, thick and lustrous, was pulled into a severe chignon. He wondered what it would look like spilling down her back. She moved gracefully, the rose silk of her dress made a rustling sound against her legs and her perfume was heady. She gave him a dubious glance.

With the door closed, the room became intimate and cozy. He paused, relished the silence, the peace, the opportunity for a moment of gentle distraction in the world of hard government business. The draperies had been drawn. The darkness in the room was broken only by a hooded desk lamp and the soft glow of firelight.

"Would you like a brandy?" she asked, moving to a sideboard.

"If you'll join me."

She smiled. "You looked very serious back there. Am I going to need it?"

"Possibly."

He should have thought before he answered. With the word, her hand, holding the decanter, halted in midair. She secured the bottom with her other hand, and he could see that both hands were shaking. "I've had the impression all evening that something was simmering just under the surface of the dinner conversation. Please tell me, is there something wrong with my father?" she asked. Her voice had dropped to a frightened plea.

"No, of course not, Selena. I give you my word."

Silently he admonished Turnus. He hadn't missed the former ambassador's anxious mood during dinner. He wasn't sure what had caused the show of nerves that was so unlike Turnus. Mentally he shrugged—only child leaving home, he supposed.

But Selena had noted it, as well, and thought her father was ailing. He took a step toward her, then halted. He felt uncertain as to how to proceed. Such feelings were alien to him.

He opened the button of his dinner jacket and thrust one hand into the pocket of his trousers. "What I have to say is personal. It is a subject to be discussed between you and me."

Her alarm turned to puzzlement. "You and me?"

Nicholas nodded to the sideboard. "Pour the brandy and let's sit down."

If thirty years ago, Turnus had taken his family back to Karastonia to live, he thought irritably, this would have been so much easier. Everything could have been arranged with a minimum of commotion.

The Karastonian practice of arranging marriages was not carried out with barbaric inflexibility, but it was common. Traditional. No Karastonian father would ever force his daughter—or son—into a distasteful alliance. But an advantageous marriage was something that the parents were responsible for providing for their children, just like food and clothing, shelter and an education. The children grew up expecting it.

And the system worked extremely well. The divorce rate in his country was one of the lowest among the Western nations.

But here in the United States he was faced with a drastically different situation. He was confronting an independent Yankee who just happened to have Karastonian blood in her veins. Instead of the calm, logical conversation he'd anticipated, instead of the cool, reasoned arguments with which he'd hoped to present his plan, he'd managed to alarm her.

Sounds registered in the silence, which only moments ago had seemed so peaceful. The light clink of the decanter against the glass, muffled footsteps on thick carpet, and quickly she was standing in front of him, holding out a heavily cut balloon glass.

Saber's hands were large and well kept, Selena noticed. And warm, she added to herself, as his fingers brushed hers. "My father doesn't really approve of women drinking anything but sherry," she said, indicative of absolutely nothing. As she released the glass she was distracted for a moment by the clean scent of his after-shave. He'd managed to defuse her worry with his quick denial and now she tried to relax, but, under the best of circumstances, relaxation wasn't easily accomplished around this man.

She settled into one of a comfortable pair of red leather chairs that flanked the fireplace. He took the other. The fire popped, the leather creaked. She was grateful that his features were in shadow. But she was also surprised to note that she didn't need to see him to be affected by his nearness.

Saber was as sexy as he'd ever been. What was his age now? Forty-two or three? Somewhere around there. She remembered his being slightly less than ten years older than her. No matter. At eighty, Nicholas Saber would be sexy.

She wondered what he wanted to discuss with her that couldn't be discussed in front of the others. But she folded her hands in her lap and waited patiently. If Saber was like the other men she'd known from her father's homeland, he'd tell her in his own time; pressing him wouldn't do a bit of good.

Nicholas took a breath. Good Lord, he'd faced diplomatic antagonists, business competitors and political rivals with a lot more assurance than he felt right now. What could she do? Say no? Then he'd just have to begin looking for someone else. No big deal, as the Americans said.

"Selena, have you ever considered marriage?" he asked, partly to break the ice, partly to give himself an additional minute to read her reaction.

His words were greeted with a soft, husky chuckle. "That's one way to open a conversation." She shook her head in amusement.

He felt his features ease into a smile.

"My father says you are a master at the unexpected diplomatic ambush, but I am neither a diplomat, nor am I a distracted prey. I have no idea what you're leading up to. Why don't you just come out with it?"

Saber deliberately set aside his glass and slouched in his chair, crossing his feet at the ankles and linking his fingers over his stomach. The position brought his face out of the shadows and allowed her a view of his expression. "I am here to ask you to become my wife."

That part had been Bree's idea. Ask, don't tell.

She laughed.

He liked her laugh, he decided. He found the sound to be like a soothing, satisfying melody.

Saber frowned again, realizing that he was noticing too much. He remained silent.

"You're not serious," she said, amused.

"I assure you, I am very serious."

She was still more amused than concerned. "But why would you ask such a thing? You don't love me."

His expression grew hard. "Of course not. Love doesn't enter into this at all. That should be clarified from the first."

The lovely smile faded from her face to be replaced with a perplexed frown. "You'll have to excuse my being so dense. I don't quite understand, I'm afraid."

She was stepping carefully, he noticed. He almost laughed—she clearly didn't want to offend him. There was plenty of her father's talent for diplomacy in her, after all. "I also find myself somewhat at a loss."

Hoping to get this over with as quickly as possible, he gave her what he hoped was a reassuring look. "You know, Selena, this is the first time I've ever proposed."

"But you've been married," she protested, her confusion mounting. Suddenly her brow cleared. And her eyes narrowed suspiciously. "Oh. That was an arranged marriage, wasn't it?"

Dangerous ground, thought Saber. Bree had also cautioned that, above all, he should *never* let Selena know that he had arranged the marriage with her father. "Most American women would be deeply offended by that sort of arrangement," Bree had said. She had then added, "You have to give her a very good reason to give up what sounds like a promising career."

"Yes, my first marriage was arranged," he said calmly. "We were both very young," he added, hoping the excuse would defuse the situation, so he could go on and give her his 'very good reason.'

She straightened in her chair. "Did my father know about this?" she demanded.

"I discussed the offer with both of your parents, yes," he answered carefully.

"Did you also know that my father once tried to arrange a marriage for me?" she demanded, those smoky gray eyes flashing.

Her anger, swift and unanticipated, seemed to have come from nowhere. Damn it, Turnus should have warned him. No wonder he'd been nervous at dinner. Saber maintained an even tone. "No, I didn't know that. Clearly you didn't appreciate his efforts."

She shot him another glare. "Of course I didn't appreciate his efforts. It is an outdated and rather insulting custom." Then she shrugged and struggled to control her annoyance. "Well, no matter. I appreciate your offer of marriage, but the answer is no."

"Is there someone else?" He spoke quickly, irritated by her instant refusal.

"No," she answered, just as quickly. "I simply don't wish to be married." She sat forward as though she were going to leave.

He'd expected her reaction. "I hope you'll hear me out," he said smoothly. "At least, give me a chance to explain my position to you. You know, Selena, that this suggestion didn't simply come out of nowhere."

She watched him warily but didn't object further. Instead she eased back in the chair and waited.

He picked up his glass again and absently swirled the amber liquid around, watching the motion. "I knew when I stood for election that the office of president would be demanding, especially since we were still feeling our way along in regard to many issues."

He sipped from his glass. "Over a year has now passed since the election. We'll soon celebrate the first anniversary of our democracy."

He hoped that he wasn't revealing too much of his weariness, but he sighed, aware that he had to be honest about his reasons if he were to have a chance of winning her acceptance. "In reality, the office of president is even more arduous than I had anticipated," he admitted wryly. "I find that I genuinely need a woman at my side. A woman like you. And not only for companionship. I need the guidance of someone with your experience. Though the birth of democracy has brought about many positive changes, it has also been a strenuous transition." During the pause that followed his words, he rose to return his glass to the bar. The brandy was potent and he was tired enough to appreciate its relaxing benefits, but he needed his wits about him. "It's been particularly difficult for the women."

Selena had her mouth open to reiterate the fact that she had no intention of accepting Saber's proposal, but at his last statement, she hesitated. "The women?"

He shrugged and returned to the chair facing her. "Men seem to take naturally to freedom. Women don't," he said carelessly.

She stared at him, unable to find words to express her wonder at this whole conversation, particularly his last, negligently offensive, comment. She shook her head helplessly.

He took the gesture for another negative and went on, "I hope you won't refuse without considering the good you could do. The women of our country—and especially the young girls, the women of tomorrow—need a strong intelligent role model." He leaned forward in his chair and rested his forearms on his knees; his urgency communicated itself to her in his posture and in the steady way his eyes met hers. "And I want—need—a wife to share my life." He paused, one corner of his mouth turning up in what might have been a small smile of regret.

Selena remembered his wife, Lisha, so beautiful, dying so young. The gossip had been that Nicholas Saber was devastated. From her own observation, she didn't doubt it for a second. That must be the reason for his statement about love not entering into this. He would never love anyone the way he had loved Lisha.

Then she had another thought. What would the people of his country—she couldn't think of it as her own, even though legally it was—think when he married again?

"So this would not be...what did they call it in Victorian times? A marriage in name only?"

"God, no! That would be a very uncomfortable situation."

Despite herself she was both flattered and stirred by his prompt denial.

"I hope you don't imagine that you have to be in love with someone to feel desire and physical enjoyment," he went on. "Love is a dangerous emotion."

She wasn't sure how to answer. Her blood warmed quickly under the deep tone of his voice and the intensity of his gaze as he let his eyes roam over her.

"I won't hurry you into bed." He exhaled heavily and sat back again. Once more the shadows claimed his face. "You must understand, Selena. I haven't lived the life of a monk and I don't intend to start now. But, if you marry me, I give you my word that I'll be faithful."

Selena sighed, linked her fingers and leaned forward, unconsciously mirroring his former posture. "Saber, I am not unaware of the honor you do me, and yours is an appealing offer." Without thinking she had slipped into the more formal cadence of continental English. "But I must answer with a definite and final no. I have a life, a career, family, here in the United States. I have no wish to leave." She spread her hands in a gesture of finality. "I'm sorry."

His eyes were black as sin, she thought, fascinated by the glare of displeasure she saw in the dark, brooding gaze. This man didn't like to lose. And then, as quickly as the expression had appeared, it vanished, making her wonder if she'd imagined it.

"I understand," he said noncommittally. Then he stood up, a signal that the conversation was over. "I suppose we should join the others."

Clearly he felt no real regret. Selena was surprised at the sting of disappointment she felt at that. "Please make my excuses to the others. I am really tired and I think I'd like to go to bed now."

"Certainly." He crossed to the door and held it open for her. "Good night, Selena."

"Good night, Saber." She paused, thinking that she might add something. But what could she say? Finally, she shook her head and left him.

Saber's brain was still functioning in another time zone. He knew he would be unable to sleep, so when he reached his room he didn't undress.

He had brought plenty of work with him but, after a few minutes, he realized that his papers weren't going to hold his attention. He thought about reading, but nothing on the shelves appealed to him. He flipped on the television, and flipped it off again. Restlessly he wandered the large bedroom.

The house was too damned quiet. From a chair, he picked up his discarded jacket and tie and stood for a moment looking down at them. Then he dropped them again.

He'd been rather surprised at his let-down feeling and had fought to keep it from showing as he'd made

Selena's excuses and carried on a conversation with the others over coffee.

Thank God none of them had dared to question him concerning the results of his interview with Selena. Considering the mood he was in, he would probably have bitten off a head or two.

Odd. He hadn't realized that her refusal would affect him in that way—in *any* way. Maybe because he hadn't expected her to refuse. Damn it, he needed her. *Karastonia* needed her, he amended.

He paced for a moment, trying to come up with an alternative. Thoughtfully, he searched his mental list of acquaintances for another woman who could fulfill all his criteria. He couldn't come up with a single one who was as appropriate as Selena.

What had happened to his celebrated powers of persuasion? he asked himself. Where were the smooth words when he needed them? Where were the diplomatic finesse, the savvy, the skill, the subtlety?

He rolled back his sleeves another notch and marched determinedly to the bookshelf. To hell with it, he thought as he pulled down a book and let it fall open in his broad hand. He'd find someone else.

He paused, book forgotten in his hand, and stared into the middle distance.

There was no avoiding it. Selena Mastron had seemed tailor-made for the role of Mrs. Nicholas Saber.

The household was quiet. Selena had heard the footsteps in the broad hallway, the soft good-nights and the closing doors, only because she was listening for them. She was wide-awake, unsettled by Saber's astonishing proposal. Unsettled, as well, by her own response to the idea. True, she had no interest in marriage, but if she did have, Nicholas Saber would certainly be a leading candidate for a husband.

She thought about the beautiful country that held a number of members of her family as well as half her allegiance. The women she had known from there were bright, cosmopolitan. Saber must be exaggerating the problem. And yet, if there was a problem, she was flattered that he thought she could be part of the solution. As a matter of fact, the more she thought about it, the more flattered she was by the whole proposal. *Nicholas Saber...*

When the telephone rang at midnight, she had almost forgotten she was expecting a call. She snatched up the extension on the table beside her bed, hoping the sound hadn't awakened anyone else.

The conversation lasted no more than a minute, then she hung up.

Had the telephone rung more than one time, Saber would have answered the extension in his room. He was accustomed to being awakened at all hours, but he wondered who in this house was expecting a call so late.

As a rule, midnight phone calls signaled an emergency.

Or they were from a lover.

Bree certainly didn't have one of those. He doubted that Jayne had ever had an unfaithful thought in her life. Which left Selena. Had she lied to him about being involved with another man? Was she even now whispering soft words of passion into the telephone?

Or was there something amiss in the household? He went to his door and listened.

Selena grumbled under her breath as she leaned into the refrigerator. Surely there was some strawberry jam; her mother *knew* she loved strawberry jam. There had always been a standing order for the stuff.

She reached to the very back, knocking over a jar of mayonnaise in the process, and brought out the only squat jar she could find. Raspberry. Well, that would have to do.

When she turned, she almost dropped the jar. Saber stood in the doorway, still dressed in his tux pants and white shirt. "Saber! You scared me."

"I'm sorry." He eyed the jar she held. "I heard the telephone."

Selena gave a fleeting thought to her own attire and then dismissed it. She'd pulled on her jeans with the faded Redskins shirt she slept in. Not glamorous but certainly modest enough. "I'm sorry it woke you. The call was for me."

He seemed to stiffen. "I was awake. A problem?" he asked casually.

She went to the drawer that held the silverware and took out a spoon. "No." She set the jar down hard and screwed off the top. Then she hooked a stool over with her bare toe and plunked herself down, anger in every aspect of her movements. "Well, yes. A co-worker called."

Van Styles had tried, but hadn't succeeded, to keep the triumph out of his voice. "I didn't get my promotion," she stated curtly.

"Ah, Selena, I'm sorry," he said. He sat on the stool across from her and folded his arms on the counter. "Your mother told me how much you had been counting on it. Aren't you going to put that on anything?" He nodded toward the spoonful of jam she was raising to her lips.

She tasted the sweet fruity mixture before she answered. Not bad. "No, I like it straight. Though I prefer strawberry. Would you like—?" She indicated the jar.

He smiled, but shuddered inwardly at the thought. "No, thank you."

They sat that way for a minute, neither of them speaking. Saber's mind was turning over the news about her job. Could he use it to his advantage? He lifted his head and what he saw sent all self-concern out of his thoughts. A couple of glistening tears hovered at the corner of her eyes.

She looked over and caught him watching her. She lifted her chin and blinked furiously to stem the tears. But the action merely served to dislodge them. They tumbled down her cheeks. "I'm sorry," she whispered, swiping at the wetness with her fingertips. "I half expected this after my last interview with the board of regents. I shouldn't let it upset me."

And that was his undoing. She looked so vulnerable. It was the first time he'd ever seen her look that way. The legs of his stool scraped the floor noisily. He circled the table and pulled her gently to her feet. "Ah, Selena, it's not worth your tears."

She felt dainty in his arms and smelled of wildflowers. Her hair was silky against his face. He held her for a long time. She was no longer crying, but she seemed to respond to his support. He ran his hand down her back to her waist and back up again.

She lifted her face and Saber couldn't resist. Without thinking, he covered her sweet naked lips with his. The kiss was brief, light. When he lifted his head to look down at her, he saw that her eyes were slightly burnished to a dark pewter color. The reaction warmed him clear through and gave him hope. She hadn't exactly returned the kiss, but she hadn't protested, either. And the kiss had affected her; he could tell by her eyes.

Selena drew out of Saber's arms, holding his gaze and searching for something to say. She appreciated his tenderness and comfort, accepted the support of his strong arms willingly, without hesitation. She couldn't deny that, but now there was this moment of stinging awareness between them as a result of the kiss. She couldn't let him think that one kiss would change things.

Before she could speak, the refrigerator kicked on, startling them both. He looked around for the source of the disturbance. Their gazes met again, clashed with a note of self-consciousness, parted.

"Do the people at the school really appreciate your talents, Selena?"

It was such an odd question that Selena laughed, a bit shakily, but she laughed, nonetheless. "Obviously not." The moment of awareness had passed, she thought with some relief as he moved back around the counter to his stool and she resumed her place across from him. It was a great deal more comfortable that way, she told herself as she plucked a tissue from a box on the counter and blew her nose.

"Then let me urge you to reconsider my proposal." He held up his hand when she would have spoken. "You don't have to answer me now, but I would ask that you think about it. I promise that if you can bring yourself to accept, you will be appreciated not only by me, but also by the people of Karastonia."

She looked at him, the automatic protest dying on her lips, and she thought about what he'd said. She hadn't really given him a fair hearing, she decided. Dangerous as it was to listen to this charismatic man, she was interested and concerned.

"Tell me more about the problems the women are facing, Saber." Surprisingly she slipped easily into the Karastonian language with its rounded vowels and softly rolled consonants.

He, too, switched languages. "This may take a while."

"And I'm sure you're tired from your long trip. I should have thought of that."

He smiled, activating the deep, sexy slash in his cheek. "I'm still on Karastonian time and that makes it early afternoon. Are you sleepy?"

That smile of his was intensely potent; she must never—ever—let herself forget the overpowering infatuation she used to have for him. Because no matter how potent, that smile was also rare—most of the time he wore a look of grim determination. "No."

Facing her across the counter he began to talk. "From the moment he began to plan toward the change in government, my cousin knew he didn't want to bring along the baggage of the past. We wanted women fully involved in the governing of the country. The vote, once it was given, would be given to everyone over the age of twenty. It was never our intention to exclude women. We encouraged registration, but it wasn't until the first elections that we discovered that most of the people who had registered were men. And that won't work in a democracy. We need to produce an informed female electorate, as well. I feel the best way is by example. As my wife, you would be a highly visible woman and good symbol of what we wish to accomplish. You have the experience of having lived in a democracy all your life. You are a teacher. And from what I hear, a good one, despite the opinion of your board."

"I might consider taking a teaching job there," she said tentatively.

He shook his head firmly. "You can teach if you like. In fact, I would encourage you to do so. But you wouldn't be as effective as a role model. If we were married, you would be much more visible, much more influential." He reached across the counter and took her hands. His own were warm and slightly rough. "I know your inclination is to refuse again. I'm not asking for an answer immediately but I'm urging you to think seriously about marrying me. The proposal may have sounded impulsive but, I assure you, it isn't. I've thought this through very carefully. I'm offering you another kind of opportunity, Selena." He released her and folded his arms on the counter. He fixed her with his sin-dark gaze. When he spoke again he was serious and sincere. "You can make an important and significant difference in our country. If I didn't believe that, I wouldn't say it."

"Why me?" Her voice was not as strong as she would have liked it to be.

"You're the perfect choice. You're Karastonian."

"I'm American, too."

"You have dual citizenship," he said.

"But *marriage,* Saber?" Selena took another spoonful of jam and switched back to English. "We're not talking about going out for a casual date."

Saber dropped his chin, closing his lips as though to hide a smile. She glared at him and cleaned the jam off the spoon. It tasted sweet in her mouth. Almost sickeningly so. When he raised his gaze again, she saw no sign of amusement.

"I realize that you and I are not very well acquainted. We would maintain separate quarters for a while, to allow ourselves time to get to know each other. I won't rush you into a physical relationship before you're ready. You are a lovely woman, Selena, and I'm very attracted to you but I realize that you can't possibly feel the same way."

Oh, no? came the unbidden thought. *I've been half in love with you since I was twelve.* Her mind reeled with reminiscences—the memory of herself as a daydreaming, besotted girl, the newspaper pictures she'd collected of the charismatic foreign minister, the dry-throated responses when they'd happened to meet— and the possibilities he was laying before her now. But a schoolgirl crush was one thing; marriage was another.

She realized suddenly that this was the explanation for the sympathetic look in Bree O'Hara's eyes. Not to mention the worry in her mother's, and the satisfaction in her father's. She wasn't sure she liked that. She replaced the top on the jar of jam. "Your Excellency..." The title had slipped out.

For the first time since he'd arrived, he laughed. The sound was rich and very masculine. Ribbons of awareness wove heat around her spine. She wondered if he realized how lusty his laugh was.

"Forget the titles, Selena. We did away with those along with the monarchy. You called me Saber before. Or—my given name is Nicholas. Will you reconsider?" he added mildly.

She was disgusted with herself; she had known that his title was obsolete. Still she didn't know what she wanted to call him. She took refuge in propriety. "Very well. I would have to have some time, however, to think it over."

"Of course." He hesitated, then went on. "If you decide to marry me, I will also make it financially worth your while." That had been Ryan's idea.

Unaccustomed to feeling as ambiguous as she had felt for the past thirty minutes or so, she was grateful for the excuse to be annoyed. "I'll give you one piece of advice for free, Saber," she said, reverting automatically to Karastonian again. She rose, keeping her expression noncommittal. "Of all the ludicrous statements I've heard during this long, long night, an offer of money is the most offensive so far. I've told you I will think about it. Now, if you'll excuse me, I'm going to my room."

Back in her bed, she closed her eyes, only to see his face swim before her. She couldn't help considering the intimate aspects of marriage to Saber. His strong mouth—how would those lips feel against hers in a really serious kiss? He would give her time, of that she had no doubt. And neither did she doubt that a physical relationship with him would be satisfying. She couldn't accept. Of course, she couldn't.

What a shame.

Chapter Three

After a sleepless night, Selena arose before six, pulled on an old bathing suit and beach robe, picked up a towel and made her way through the silent house.

The brass handle under her hand was cold as she let herself out through the French doors of her father's study; the early-morning air hit her bare skin with a chilly, but not unpleasant, bite. Though the darkness was already ebbing in the east, a few of the brightest stars still winked in the western sky.

The pool would be heated, though; even this early in the season her mother swam every day. She paused at the edge of the patio, then sprinted the last twenty yards, shedding her robe as she reached the edge of the coping, and jumped in, feet first.

She came up laughing. Lord, it was colder than she'd expected. She struck out toward the far end of the pool with a vigorous stroke.

She had done as Saber had asked; she had considered carefully—all night long. But, no matter what, she couldn't see herself as his wife. This morning she would have to tell him so. Maybe.

But first she would swim laps, a lot of laps. Perhaps the cold shock of the water temperature would jump start her brain and wash away this absurd and uncharacteristic indecision. Maybe the exercise would clear out the tension which seemed to have been building within her all night. And maybe she would find a calm and firm reason to convince herself, so there would be no mistaking her determination.

Nicholas watched Selena from his bedroom window. Her body, even in the old tank suit, was superb. He mused once more about how different she was from what he'd expected.

He had returned to his room last night, confident that, although he'd made a blunder at the end, he'd reasserted his diplomatic finesse somewhat. He'd been clumsy in his first attempt after dinner—perhaps too sure of himself. When she'd turned him down flat, it had surprised him, not pleasantly. At the same time, he'd accepted that he needed to reevaluate his efforts. He'd done much better with the second opportunity.

The atmosphere in the kitchen had been more informal, and informality always helped. Every good diplomat knew that more was accomplished on the cocktail circuit than around the meeting table. The call from her school, which had left her depressed and vulnerable, hadn't hurt his case, either.

Yet, he had a premonition that in the full light of morning, Selena would again refuse, this time unequivocally.

Damn. If there weren't so many restrictions on his time he could have eased her into this idea of marriage. Last night she was tired and worried, not at all in the mood for a proposal like his. He should have known she'd turn him down flat the first time. Talking her into putting off her decision, into thinking about it for a while, hadn't been easy.

And then he'd ruined it all by his offer of money—though he still wasn't sure why.

What else could he do to convince her?

Unbidden, his subconscious suddenly suggested a fairly intriguing idea. He considered for a minute, then dismissed it. While it might appeal to her, it would be offensive to him. But the idea kept pushing at his mind, demanding to be given consideration.

It might work. At least it would give him the time he needed. And it would give her the out she needed to save her pride, autonomy, whatever it was that made American women so damned independent. He chided himself for the adjective. Her independence, "damned" or not, was just what he and his country needed at this time.

Five minutes later, Nicholas strolled to the edge of the pool and watched as Selena swam toward the far end, turned with one smooth movement, disappearing beneath the water for a moment. When she surfaced again, she resumed her long even strokes, her arms pale and smooth in the early-morning light.

Selena had seen him immediately. It was a tribute to her experience that she hadn't suddenly floundered in the water. She maintained the smooth, demanding rhythm of her strokes, but her senses were tumbling out of control.

She'd never seen Saber in jeans before. In fact, she'd never seen him in anything except a business suit or formal attire. Even last night in the kitchen without his jacket he'd still maintained his air of formality.

She had always considered him a remarkably handsome man. Dressed casually, he was devastating. He stood, legs planted apart, hands tucked into the back pockets of the jeans, watching her. In the dress shirt, the same one from last night, now badly wrinkled, his shoulders appeared twice as broad, his forearms twice as muscular.

She finished the lap in the shallow end of the pool and when her feet touched the bottom she stood slowly, keeping her back to him. She climbed the steps and, moving nonchalantly, reached down to scoop up her robe and towel. Robe belted, towel wrapped around her wet hair, she felt ready to confront him.

They stood, facing each other across the water, for a long minute. The surface, disturbed by her activity, calmed, settled into its natural drift.

"Would you like to swim?" she asked finally breaking the silence. "I'm sure there's a suit in the cabana."

"No, thank you. I came out to apologize."

She shrugged. "Apology accepted."

"I'd also like to talk to you."

Blunt to the end, thought Selena. Well, she could be just as blunt. "We've already talked, Nicholas. I thought you wanted me to think this over."

"One or two things have occurred to me. They would be advantages, I believe, from your point of view. Things that might—" He stopped, oddly at a loss.

"Sweeten the pot?" she said evenly.

He hesitated over the idiom but it only took a second for him to grasp her meaning. His lips thinned in annoyance. "I didn't mean to insult you when I offered to pay you a salary. As my wife, you will be performing many services for the country. Why shouldn't you be compensated?"

"Good God, Saber." She spun away, heading for the house but her course intersected his and his legs were longer. He caught her arm as she tried to pass.

"What is the matter with you, Selena? I'm only offering—"

"To *pay* me. Like—like a woman off the street." She tried to free her arm.

"No! You can't think that! You would be paid for your educational expertise, for your service to the women of our country, not for sharing my bed. Selena, you can't have thought—" At that he grabbed her other arm and brought her to within inches of his body.

She caught her breath. His gaze dropped to her mouth. Time seemed to hang suspended between them. He was warm, his body radiating heat. She suddenly felt an urge to warm herself in his arms, to seek comfort there as she had done last night. She couldn't control the shiver that went through her, and he noticed.

"You must be cold." He dropped his hands and his voice was heavy. "Let's finish this discussion inside over a cup of coffee."

She led the way to the back door and kept right on through to the hall. "I'm going to get dressed." She had made it to the second step leading upstairs, when she realized he was following her. She stopped. "I won't keep you waiting long, I promise."

But he wouldn't wait. "Selena, what I wanted to say was this." He raked his fingers through his hair in a gesture of frustration. "I've been trying to look at this from your point of view. And I don't want to force you into a situation where you will feel caged or imprisoned. So I've come up with another idea. We can put a time limit on this arrangement. If, after a certain period—say, a year—you don't feel that our marriage has a chance, I will arrange for you to divorce me."

Selena looked at him for a minute, wondering what it had cost him to make such an offer. She had an idea that it was a lot. At last, she nodded silently and turned away. As she headed up the stairs she felt his gaze on her back. She had the strangest feeling that— no matter how this situation was resolved—something, tentatively and potentially precious, had been lost forever.

By the time she returned to the dining room her father had made an appearance. She poured coffee for herself and joined the two men at the breakfast table.

Turnus was unusually reserved and Selena soon realized that Saber had made her father aware of what had passed between them. She should be annoyed but for some reason she was not. He'd discussed his proposal with her parents. She supposed that the parents should also be apprised of the consequences of said proposal.

With her father's next statement, however, she realized how wrong she was. Clearly Saber hadn't told the whole story. "We are all to attend a dinner at the Karastonian Embassy this evening." He laughed under his breath. "Nicholas attracts the media like honey attracts flies, and there is bound to be speculation. With your mother and I along, it would give the press a chance to get used to seeing you without questioning your presence."

"That is, of course, if you will agree to let me escort you." Saber's words drew Selena's attention and she met his even gaze. He was giving her an opportunity to say no.

Turnus seemed to be under the impression that this was a done deal but Saber knew better, thought Selena sourly. She opened her mouth to contradict her father's assumption, but Saber spoke instead. "It isn't necessary for Selena to go unless she wishes."

Go with him to an official function? That made things seem awfully definite. "I'd love to go," she said perversely. Then she wondered why.

Saber didn't hesitate. "Fine. We'll leave at seven."

Bree and Ryan joined them then and there was no chance for more conversation.

Selena was late. She had tried on and discarded several dresses before she finally decided on a blue-gray chiffon which was an old favorite of hers. She kept most of her formal things here. Aside from the occasional command performance at the home of the college president, most of her socializing at school was casual. With its classic cut and simplicity, the blue dress gave her self-confidence to meet whatever lay in store for her tonight.

She had arranged her hair in a looser chignon than she usually wore and pulled several strands free to brush her neck. Now she clasped a small but glittering blue butterfly in the arrangement.

She examined the effect, turning her head from side to side. This was ridiculous. Trying to make herself look like a romantic heroine for a man who had to have half a screw loose. Butterflies, for heaven's sake. At thirty-four she was much too old to wear butterflies in her hair. She pulled the pins from her hair and reached for her hairbrush. She was going to make them all late. What a way to start— She broke off the thought. To start what?

Nothing, she told herself. This wasn't the start of anything.

When Selena descended the staircase five minutes later, Saber caught his breath. Her glorious hair, dark as midnight, was caught up away from her face on one side by a tiny sparkling butterfly no larger than his thumb. The rest of her hair spilled down her back in loose, easy curls. His fingers literally itched to touch the silky mass. She was wearing a smoky blue, soft, floaty gown that drifted around her legs when she moved. The effect was arresting. He wished he *could* find something to criticize.

From the moment this morning when she'd left him standing at the foot of this same staircase, he'd looked for a limitation, a shortcoming in this woman. Because, as he'd gazed down into her face, framed by the damp towel, without a smidgen of make-up, he had suddenly and inexplicably grown warm and aroused. He'd quickly tried to distract himself, explaining the idea he'd come up with to put a time limit on their arrangement. As she'd climbed the stairs, though, he'd had the feeling that he had somehow made another serious mistake.

Not offering the time limit, but in the selection, itself. Selena created too many extraordinary emotions within him.

Too late; he'd already asked. But, he was beginning to suspect, this woman could have an effect on him emotionally and that was the last thing he wanted. He had stood there like a slab of wood, watching her climb the stairs in her bare feet and he had wondered if it wouldn't be better if she turned him down. Now, as he watched her descend that same staircase, looking so very different, he was almost sure of it.

The rest of the party was frozen into silence by her appearance. For some reason the fact annoyed him even further.

"I hope I haven't made us late," she said when she reached the bottom of the stairs.

She didn't rush with her apology, he noticed, wryly. She knew she was late but like all the beautiful women he'd known, she expected to be forgiven.

"Not at all," he said smoothly. "The car is waiting. Shall we go?"

The reporters had gathered outside the gate to the Karastonian Embassy. How in the world they found out he was here was always a mystery to him. As the car turned in, he could hear the shouted questions. Cameras were thrust against the window of the limo, their flashes momentarily blinding those inside. But the driver and the guards assigned to the gates knew their jobs and soon the car drew up to the chancellery entrance. The ambassador was waiting at the foot of the steps. He was alone.

Nicholas bit off a frustrated curse. This was what he was battling. Damn it, he'd sent a prescript to all the embassies. He hadn't worded it too strongly, of course, but had merely made a suggestion that the women should begin to take their places beside their husbands, greeting the guests of the country.

The world was so complicated these days. The women of Karastonia had to step forward and take their places beside the men if there was to be any hope for the democratic government to succeed. He knew they were capable of doing anything they wanted to do. He also knew that their fathers, brothers, husbands, needed to encourage them. That was another problem.

He deliberately paused after he emerged from the car to assist Selena. With a hand at her elbow, he shortened his steps to keep her even with him.

Selena could see the surprise on the face of her host. She knew exactly what Saber was doing; she was half-Karastonian, after all. She had observed the traditions and customs of the country firsthand.

"I hope your wife is not ill," said Saber when they reached the ambassador. His voice could have frozen hot fudge.

"No, sir. I mean—" The man fumbled for a minute more. Then he turned and motioned toward the door. His wife, a rather plain woman who knew her place—was standing submissively in the background. At her husband's gesture she hesitated for a second, then came forward. "We're honored to welcome you, Mr. President."

Saber charmed them both, presenting Selena as though she were the honored guest here tonight. She wasn't particularly enamored of being the subject of his object lesson, but she smiled to herself, understanding what the demonstration was meant to convey and applauding his sincere intent.

She had been unnerved by the reporters at the gates, had seen the muscle in Saber's jaw jump once in reaction to the clamor. For the first time the magnitude of his responsibility dawned on her. He was determined to wrest a democracy from the remnants of a monarchy, to turn a patriarchal society into a strong, modern nation, ready to take its place among the other democracies of the world. His was a formidable task.

She had a chance to study him briefly as the introductions were performed. If anyone could do it, she decided, he could. And then all chance for speculation was lost as they entered the building. The party was a large one. She realized immediately that the reporters at the gate were the foot soldiers. The big guns were here inside. Among the approximately one hundred and fifty guests, she counted one anchor, two newspaper correspondents, including one whose regular beat was the State Department, a well-known producer-star of a weekly television interview program, and the president of a network.

Saber accepted two glasses of champagne from the waiter; handed one to Selena and waded into the melee, keeping her by his side. He milled about. He spoke to people as though he had all the time in the world. He knew everyone here, called most by their first names, asked about everyone in their families, down to—it seemed to Selena—a mother's aunt's uncle's first cousin, twice removed. "How do you do it? I've forgotten most of the names already," she murmured once in an aside.

He grinned, a most un-Saberlike expression. "Practice, practice, practice. Isn't that how it goes?" The grin faded and he added, "I'm a politician, after all."

She was surprised by his teasing. In the car it had been obvious that something had happened to annoy him and it appeared to have something to do with her. The tension had been so thick it could be cut with a knife. At first she'd thought he was irritated because she had been slow in getting downstairs, but she knew she hadn't been more than a minute or two behind her mother and father.

"You seem to have learned your trade well."

He shrugged. "I've known most of these people for many years."

She also knew a few people here, leftovers from the days when her father had been the ambassador. As the bids for Saber's attention increased, she realized that her presence was slowing him down. When she saw the U.S. Secretary of Commerce edging purposefully toward them, she touched his sleeve. "You don't have to baby-sit me, Saber. I'll be all right on my own."

He looked around dubiously, then nodded. "This trade agreement I'm here to discuss with your Department of Commerce is important, and there are some people I should speak with. But don't go far away,'' he said, his gaze intensifying as he looked down at her. For a mere fleeting instant they looked into each other's eyes and the time seemed to stretch as the room receded from around them.

At last Selena interrupted the spell. "I won't,'' she said, wondering about the breathlessness in her voice.

Not more than a moment had passed, surely, when she felt, rather than saw, the curious members of the press begin to move in on her. Nothing overt—they were here as guests and behaved properly. But they were, after all, journalists. The network anchor reached her first.

The questions were polite but probing and finally the producer-star of the weekly television news program came right out and asked what they had all wanted to ask. "Are you and Saber an item?''

"I don't know what you mean,'' she answered calmly. She wasn't about to make this easy for the man.

"Saber has quite a reputation. He's dated a number of American women. I just wondered if you were his latest.'' The man's expression was almost sneering.

"Saber and his friends are spending the weekend at my parents' home in Virginia,'' she answered with dignity. "We are all his guests. As are you, I believe.''

Mercifully, dinner was announced. She looked around to see Saber making his way through the crowd toward her.

"That reporter's tie must be too tight—it seems to have cut off the flow of blood to his brain,'' said Bree's voice from behind her.

Selena laughed.

"What's funny?" asked Ryan.

Saber reached her side. He lifted a brow and looked from Bree to Selena.

Bree linked her arms with her husband's. "You don't have to worry about this one, Saber. She can handle herself."

Selena wondered how long Bree had been standing behind her while she talked to the journalists.

As the evening progressed, Saber realized that he was again searching for a flaw in Selena. He chastised himself for the effort. There was much to be admired in this woman. She handled the curious and the speculative with equal aplomb.

He, on the other hand, needed to get his temper under control. As if he didn't have enough on his mind, the trade agreement he had come here to sign was in jeopardy. There had been pressure on the United States, from a country much more powerful than Karastonia, not to sign the treaty as it was written.

His country desperately needed this agreement. When he'd inquired, the U.S. Secretary of Commerce had reassured him about the president's commitment to sign, but he wasn't encouraged. He knew the havoc politics could play.

After dinner they were first entertained by a classical violinist. Selena listened to the brilliant performance with only half her attention. The other half was focused on Saber. She had watched his expression grow more serious with each passing hour until lines of strain were deeply etched around his eyes and mouth.

He'd disappeared twice during the entertainment for brief intervals—one time with the ambassador, another time with a group of people that included her father and the Secretary of Commerce.

Both times, when he'd returned, Saber's visage had been a bit blacker. Whether from aggravation or apprehension, she couldn't tell, but clearly something was wrong. She felt a swell of compassion for him and sympathy for his position. He couldn't even enjoy an evening out without being badgered by his responsibilities.

At last, a pianist concluded the final performance to enthusiastic applause. Saber slipped back into place beside her just before the lights came up. She turned to him with a smile as she clapped her hands.

There was no logical explanation for what happened next. As the illumination grew gradually brighter, he looked down at her, a perfunctory smile on his lips. And suddenly, to her astonishment, as though the mere sight of her was somehow comforting, the lines in his face eased, his troubled expression relaxed, his dark eyes, which had been clouded with worry, miraculously cleared. The token smile became a grin of genuine pleasure.

"Was he good?" he whispered.

"*She* was terrific," she answered, and almost laughed aloud as Saber did a comical double take.

Then he gave her a rueful smile. "Sorry. That was unforgivable. Thank you for saving me embarrassment."

She felt warmed to her toes by the change. For the first time she began to reflect on the possibility that she could help, that her solace and support might be of value to this man. It was a startling thought.

He carried heavy burdens. Did she imagine she could do anything to ease them? Did she want to? It gave her a lot to think about.

The moment was interrupted by the Karastonian national anthem and they all rose to honor the flag. They said their goodbyes and the limousine was brought around.

"I shall await your convenience tomorrow, Mr. President," said the ambassador.

Saber was standing beside the open door of the car. The rest to them were inside but Selena could hear him plainly.

"I'll be here early tomorrow morning. Move the first meeting up from Monday to tomorrow night. If that is possible."

"I am sure I can arrange it."

Saber nodded and shook the man's hand. He climbed in beside her and the limousine started down the curved driveway.

Jayne and Bree were discussing the evening. Turnus and Ryan were arguing good-naturedly about the merits of living in Boston versus Washington.

"I didn't realize that you would be leaving so soon," said Selena softly. Her words, under the conversation of the other four, were inaudible except to his ears. It seemed she wouldn't have as much time as she thought to mull over the events of the evening.

"I had planned to stay until Monday morning but we have discovered an unexpected obstacle to the trade agreement I was to sign. It will take some effort to straighten out the difficulties.''

''I understand. I'd like to talk to you before you leave.''

Saber looked sharply at her. He was struck by the quickening of his pulse, but he could read nothing from her expression. ''Shall we have a brandy when we get back to your parents' house?''

''That would be fine,'' she answered.

Selena linked her fingers in her lap and waited for Saber to pour the brandy. There was no fire tonight and the room seemed chilly.

Then he was standing before her, his hand extended with the balloon glass in it. ''Thank you.''

Saber looked down at her face. She was outwardly composed but, he noticed, she turned the glass in her hands not even aware that she was doing it. He waited.

She sipped from the glass and set it aside. ''Saber,'' she said, hesitating. She had to crane her neck to look up at him. ''Please, sit down.''

A faint smile played around his lips as he took the chair across from her. She looked like she was waiting for the hangman.

She took a long breath. ''Well, Saber, with certain conditions, I am prepared to accept your proposal.''

A light flared briefly in his eyes. He sat back in the chair and folded his arms across his broad chest. ''You seem nervous.''

''Well, what do you expect? Of course I'm nervous. And not completely convinced that I'm doing the right thing.''

Saber hid a smile. He'd not seen her nervous before. "What are the conditions?" he asked, intrigued.

"Well, I couldn't leave until after school is out for the summer."

He nodded thoughtfully and continued to struggle to keep the smile off his face. He'd never heard her preface a sentence with "well" and now he'd heard three. Obviously indicative of a certain state of mind. When they were married it would be a useful fact to know. "When is that?"

"The third of June." She watched him warily.

"And did you feel that I would object? Selena, I am not unreasonable." He leaned forward and took the glass from her. Then he gripped her hands between his. His voice lowered as he tried to convey his satisfaction. "You won't regret your decision, Selena. I'd like to take you home with me when I leave on Wednesday, but I understand that you have a commitment to your position at the school," he said gently.

She seemed to draw some comfort from his attitude. "Saber, I would also hope—and I want us to promise—that we be honest with each other. You said that if I wasn't happy, I could..." She paused.

"You could divorce me," he finished for her. "And I meant that, Selena. You will always be free to leave and I will make it as easy as possible for you."

She squeezed his hands. "And I want you to have that freedom, as well, Saber. If you aren't happy with our bargain, I want you to tell me. I couldn't stand it if we weren't honest with each other. You may find someone someday that you may be able to love. Please promise to tell me, Saber."

His features hardened again at the mention of the word. "Very well. If you need me to say it, I will. I promise to be honest with you, Selena."

She inhaled and smiled. "Thank you. And I accept your proposal."

A corner of his mouth turned up. "Thank you, Selena."

The bargain was sealed, not with a kiss, but with a handshake.

Chapter Four

The head of the history department, Dr. Wrens, summoned Selena to his office for the second time in a week. As she waited in the anteroom, she was well aware of the looks she was getting from her colleagues as they passed through the office on their way to classes, to their homes, to conferences. She was getting looks from everybody these days—the students, the janitor, the man who filled the soft-drink machine. Ever since her picture had appeared in *USA Today*—one of those taken through the window of the limousine—she seemed to be fair game for whispered speculation and long assessing stares, even from her friends. So far, she'd managed to escape the cover pictures of the tabloids, but that would probably be next.

Sometimes, despite her determined demeanor, she

wanted to shriek. Was she becoming paranoid? No, actually she was simply mad as hell.

She maintained her expression of calm and congeniality when the secretary called her name. "Dr. Mastron, Dr. Wrens is ready for you."

She smiled. "Thank you."

As she passed the young woman's desk, she caught the wink, the grin, the crossed fingers.

Somehow she kept herself from doing or saying anything rash. Earlier in the week when she'd been called in to this same office, she'd had to endure the girl's gushing congratulations on her engagement, the knowing and rather surprisingly cunning look, the outlandish but probing questions that stopped short of asking how her fiancé was in bed. But not very far short.

She continued to be shocked at the almost-indecent curiosity that surrounded the life of Nicholas Saber.

Her father seemed to want to reassure her, calling every night to explain that this kind of thing didn't go on in Karastonia. Clearly, Turnus was afraid that his daughter, a mercurial mixture of two divergent cultures, would lose patience and call the whole thing off.

In reality, the tempest served to strengthen her determination. If she decided to call off this marriage, it wouldn't be over something as trivial as overly enthusiastic journalists.

"Have a seat, Dr. Mastron," said Dr. Wrens as Selena entered the room.

His head was bent over some papers. He didn't bother to look up or to rise. She sat across the desk and pondered his shiny bald spot. At last he raised his head and pinned her with his bright blue eyes. "What are we going to do about this situation, Dr. Mastron?''

"I don't know, sir," answered Selena honestly.

"The distinguished gentlemen of the press are causing some rather complicated problems for the school."

And for me, thought Selena, thinking of the gamut she had to run to get inside her home in the evenings, of the telephone that rang constantly.

And the mail was voluminous. Some of the letters were official and congratulatory but many more were from acquaintances, even strangers, asking for money or intervention.

But the man across the desk seemed to have no perception of the problems she might face. He certainly gave no sign of sympathy or understanding. "The distinguished gentlewomen are causing their share of problems, as well," she observed mildly.

The look he gave her was puzzled and she had to bite her lip to keep from laughing out loud. Even now, he didn't get the point.

"Since we have your resignation in hand, the dean has suggested that I get in touch with Daniel Summers, to see if he can finish out this term for you.

Selena became very still. Here it was, then. She had handed in her resignation, effective the end of this term, but they wanted her out immediately. Dr. Daniel Summers had retired from teaching. He lived in a nearby community, however, and he had filled in when flu had devastated the college faculty this past fall.

Selena had thought she was reconciled to her decision but the idea of severing all contact with this place suddenly made her feel very sad and melancholy. She had many good friends here; she'd enjoyed her work. It was difficult to remember the frustrations or the irritations at a time like this. And the thought of leaving it behind forever made her very sad.

The long-distance telephone connection was so clear that Saber might have been in the next room. Still, he didn't seem to understand. He had been silent since she'd told him seconds ago that she had been asked to leave the campus because of the commotion engendered by the announcement of their engagement. "Did you hear me, Saber? I've been fired, axed, dismissed."

He chuckled. He actually chuckled!

If he *had* been in the next room she would have choked him. Was he really so unfeeling? What had she gotten herself into? "Saber," she said quietly. "I am not in the best of moods and I find nothing in the least amusing about this situation."

"I was laughing at my own blunder, not at you, Selena," he said calmly. "I apologize for not listening to your warning against an immediate announcement of our engagement. I admit I was wrong not to foresee this." He paused. "Anyway, thank you for not saying, 'I told you so,'" he added.

She had reluctantly agreed when he wanted to make the announcement before he left the United States. She had joined him at the embassy the last day before he returned to Karastonia. There had been a small engagement party. No press. It had been very pleasant.

She was slightly mollified by his apology. "That would serve no purpose."

"You are being very generous. This must be a difficult predicament. Especially when you have to deal with it all alone." He stopped for a moment. "I'll wind up a few things here and be there tomorrow or the next day. Thursday at the latest."

Had he missed her? His voice had certainly grown low and intimate with the last few words, sending shivers down her spine, setting up tiny explosions of warmth at her nape. It was a lover's voice, and she was as stunned by her own reaction as she was by the offer.

She had missed him more than she'd expected during the past few weeks. Or was she only impatient to get this thing done, now that it had been decided?

"That isn't necessary," she said quickly. "I just wanted you to know that I'll be at my parents' house. I'm leaving as soon as I can arrange an appointment with the movers." With regret, she looked around her apartment, at all the things she'd collected over the past ten years.

"Leave it all, Selena. You needn't be bothered with such details. I'll take care of everything."

It was a tempting offer. Leave everything to him, let him hire the movers, deal with the lease. She could make one more trip—this one to her car, suitcase in hand—and drive away from the problem.

She collected her thoughts, overcoming the temptation. "Saber, the reason you hired me for this job—"

"Hired?" He erupted in anger. "Selena, you are going to be my wife!"

"Will you be quiet and listen?" she demanded, not unkindly, but firmly.

Deathly silence followed her words. She sensed his struggle with himself over the thousands of miles that separated them. His irritation seemed to bounce off the telephone satellite and into her living room. She would be willing to bet that no woman had ever spoken to him like that. She could speak firmly now because she wasn't tied to him. The idea of what his reaction would be when she was, brought on a moment's trepidation.

"Saber, you want me to set an example for the women of Karastonia. You selected me because I'm able to function independently, because I don't have to depend on anyone to solve all my problems. Now, if you won't let me handle this situation on my own, I'll have to presume you didn't mean any of it. And in that case we may as well call this off right now."

"Blackmail, Selena?"

"No," she said immediately. "Not at all. Just a reminder of the reasons for this marriage."

Another pause, which may or may not have been a satellite time delay, he said, "How long will you need? Surely you agree that there is no further need to postpone your coming to Karastonia."

"Yes," she said slowly. "I do agree, but perhaps we should stick to our timetable. It will take me a month or six weeks, at least, to wind things up here. Besides packing and moving, I want to go to New York to do some shopping."

"I'll give you a week to pack. We can stop in Paris for you to shop."

Good Lord, didn't the man hear a word she said? "Saber, I don't *want* to shop in Paris. I want to shop in New York. Three weeks."

"Ten days."

She sighed and held the telephone away from her ear to glare at it. Then she sighed again. "Ten days," she said finally.

The ten-day deadline stretched to two unbelievably hectic weeks. Even so, if it hadn't been for her mother's help, she would never have accomplished everything even then. Now they were all packed, the bags were loaded into the limousine, which had arrived a short time ago bearing her fiancé.

Selena was waiting with Jayne in the drawing room when Saber and her father came out of the study.

Turnus wore a beaming smile. He looked better than he had looked in some time. His color was good and his step had more spring in it. "Ready to leave?" he asked Selena unnecessarily.

She had no idea what had caused the last-minute delay but she smiled back and said, "Yes." If her smile was a little uneven around the edges, no one seemed to notice.

The chauffeur waited. Turnus and Jayne entered the car first. As Selena started to join them, she looked back one last time at her childhood home. She'd agreed to this undertaking, this venture into the unknown, but the actual leave-taking was more than a bit daunting.

It was silly of her, she knew, but Selena was hit with the sudden and unexpected temptation to run upstairs and hide in her room.

As though he could read her thoughts, Saber put a supportive hand at her back, surprising her. She met his dark, unsmiling gaze for a moment.

Suddenly his expression softened. His smile was warm and self-confident, making her feel slightly better. "I almost forgot something." He leaned into the open door. "One minute," he said to her parents and took her arm. He turned her away from the car. "Come with me."

They reached the dappled shade of a willow tree a few yards from the drive. Saber reached into his pocket and withdrew a small velvet-covered box.

Selena gaped when he withdrew a ring, dropped the box back in his pocket and reached for her left hand. "Good heavens, Saber."

The flawless diamond was blue-white, and as big as a cherry from George Washington's renowned tree— if there was such a tree. Historically speaking, there had always been some question about the legend. Surrounding the large stone were rubies the size of cherry pits. "Good heavens," she repeated weakly as he slid the thing onto her finger.

She had tried to convince Saver that it wasn't necessary for him to fly all the way to the United States to accompany her and her parents to Karastonia. But he'd insisted, determination hardening his voice each time she protested. It was almost as though he read hesitation in their telephone conversations and expected her to change her mind. Now he placed the ring on her finger with the same determination. It was a perfect fit.

"Thank you. It's beautiful." She forced a sincere smile. "Truly breathtaking." For someone who rarely wore jewelry, except for a utilitarian watch and her grandmother's pearls, the ring would take some getting used to. Luckily she was tall and her fingers were long, so the proportion wasn't *too* unfortunate.

"It was my mother's," he said as he looked down into her face. He hesitated, as though he wanted to say something more. But he simply gripped her fingers, and when he did speak she had an idea that the words weren't what he'd planned to say.

"I'm honored that you've agreed to marry me, Selena."

She searched his features, hoping for more. They hadn't had a moment alone since he'd arrived early this morning, looking extremely weary after flying all night. But after a brief hesitation, he simply smiled, touched her back lightly and gestured toward the waiting car.

The drive was over too quickly, the airport red tape eliminated too easily, and all at once it was time to board the huge private jet that would take her to live in a foreign land.

It didn't matter that she held dual citizenship; she still considered herself an American. And she was leaving her country to marry a foreigner. She was going to spend the rest of her life somewhere else.

Saber watched Selena climb on board the plane. Her carriage was exquisitely straight. He noticed that the heels she wore caused her hips to move with fluid grace under the smooth fabric of her skirt. She carried the jacket of her royal blue suit over her arm and her soft blouse, an almost colorless cream, draped enticingly over her breasts. Her raven-black hair was twisted neatly into a chignon. He wondered if she'd packed the tiny butterfly clip.

Her expression was serene, but he hadn't missed the panic in her eyes when she'd turned for a last look at her parents' home. He felt a certain sympathy, but he couldn't help her with this. Leaving home was an emotional experience that she'd have to handle on her own.

He wouldn't be of much help to her, period, over the next couple of weeks. His own schedule, in preparation for a honeymoon trip—which wouldn't be a honeymoon at all, he thought wryly—was filled to capacity except for the formal festivities surrounding the wedding.

He was half expecting her to change her mind, which she could do. In spite of the engagement ring she wore, until he put the official wedding ring on her finger, she wasn't his.

Even afterward, she wouldn't really be his for another year. He'd given her a promise of freedom and that was the time they'd agreed on. He had a year to convince her that this marriage could work, that what she could offer her Karastonian counterparts was worth the sacrifice of the life she was leaving behind.

The plane was cleared for takeoff and, as the engines revved noisily to achieve maximum power, Saber thought about the change his own feelings had undergone in regard to his intended bride. Now that the decision had been made, he was surprised at his impatience to get this done and to make her his wife, to settle into, if not a conventional marriage, at least a certain domestic routine. The prospect filled him with the first contented pleasure he'd felt in a long, long time.

He was as sick as she was of the publicity, the notoriety surrounding this marriage. When she'd called from the school two weeks ago, he hadn't exactly been surprised. In fact, he'd been expecting a call every day, expecting her to inform him that she had changed her mind, so it was with some relief that he listened to her story of being asked to leave.

He had read the papers and watched television, and he had seen the pictures. Selena entering the stone buildings on the campus where she taught. Selena thrusting her way through the crowd of reporters at her condominium complex. Selena, looking unhappy but indomitable. She was getting a firsthand view of his onstage life-style. He'd been expecting her to back out. He'd wondered if he could blame her. Several times he'd also wondered if he didn't want her to do just that.

Gradually, as he'd watched her or read about her movements, he'd begun to realize that this woman was not one to walk away because of pressure. Slowly his admiration grew for her poise, her tact, her equilibrium. She was really an exceptional woman; he had chosen well.

But the very fact made him pause, made him wonder about his own ability to resist an emotional involvement.

He was proud of her for showing such spirit. She would have to draw on that strength often over the next days because the situation wouldn't soon get any better. The interest in this wedding among Karastonians—indeed among all Europeans—was, if anything, more intense. Before they arrived in his country he should try to prepare her for what would happen.

Her picture was splashed on shop fronts and in windows. The wedding was the biggest event in the small country since the monarchy had been abolished and they'd held their first elections. The people were elated that their president had chosen a wife—a second wife.

The romantics among them were demanding to know the intimate details of Selena's life. What she would wear when she arrived, what her life in the United States had been like, what she would wear at the state dinner, who styled her hair, what her students thought of her, what she would wear to be married, who her lovers had been. The last had given Saber pause. He wondered about that himself.

The skeptics of Karastonia, on the other hand, had speculated as to her role as their first lady and questioned her allegiance to her father's land.

The media had demanded interviews, background material, an official portrait. The last had caused a few problems, but finally her father had convinced her to sit for a well-known photographer while she was shopping in New York. That was the picture that now graced the streets and byways of his country.

In Saber's mind the formal portrait wasn't Selena. It displayed her likeness, but it didn't reflect the energy or the intelligence within her.

When they reached cruising altitude, he unfastened his seat belt and got to his feet. "Would you like to look around?" he asked.

She searched his features, her eyes wide with an elusive emotion, and then glanced across the aisle toward her parents. "Yes, I would."

Turnus and Jayne seemed to understand his need to be alone with Selena for a few minutes because they didn't follow. Their comments on the engagement ring had been restrained, if slightly awed.

He showed her the office space behind the cockpit, where his secretary was at work, and the cockpit itself. He introduced her to the crew. Finally he led her to the rear of the aircraft where there was a private stateroom and bath.

"It's very luxurious, isn't it?" Selena said in response to Saber's explanation of the plush facilities.

"The government inherited the plane from my cousin. Along with his yacht and the palace, of course."

She knew the palace from the days of the king, and she didn't relish the idea of living there at all. After the monarchy was abolished, the building had been quickly remodeled. Saber had described the changes; but, even refurbished inside, the exterior was certain to be the formal place she remembered. The office of the president and other administrative offices had been incorporated into the design, as well as the elaborate facilities for formal entertaining, and the living quarters for the president. So she would be compelled to live in the huge forbidding edifice, for now at least. "I see."

Her voice sounded wooden even to herself. Couldn't he understand how unsettled she was feeling? She needed more than a tour of the plane, more than a recitation of the luxuries that would accompany her position; she needed reassurance. She needed personal conversation; she needed a sense of connection and cohesion and contact of some kind. Maybe then this wouldn't all seem so artificial and awkward. She turned to face him.

"Where is the king living now?" she asked. Anything to start a conversation.

"He has a lodge in the mountains and a house in the city and he travels."

"Do you think he's happy with his decision?"

Saber looked off into the middle distance for a minute, thoughtfully. "You know, Selena, he's seventy years old. Before the change in government he looked frail and tired. Now he looks ten years younger. He has more time for reading. He even plays cards with old friends." He smiled absently. "He has begun using a health club...and he's more content than I've ever seen him."

"I'm glad," said Selena softly. "He's a wonderful man." She hesitated. "Saber, I—"

"Selena—" They spoke simultaneously. His smile was rueful. "You first."

Whatever she'd been planning to say went out of her head as she looked into his dark eyes. She'd never noticed the golden glints in their depths. She was mesmerized into silence.

Saber couldn't have missed her reaction. He smiled and touched her cheek.

The contact was electric. It brought her to her senses. Well, she'd wanted contact, hadn't she? "I'm not exactly sure what I want to say or how to say it. It's very difficult."

He took her hand. "Then let me say it for you. You've had a glimpse of what being married to me will be like and you don't relish the experience."

She smiled. "That's part of it," she admitted. She sat on the edge of the bed and traced the design of the spread with a fingernail. "How in the world do you abide all the media attention?"

He joined her on the bed, sitting sideways with his back to the cabin door. "I'm hoping marriage will temper their enthusiasm," he said, smiling.

She frowned.

"Selena." His voice was very low, but unemotional.

She met his gaze questioningly.

"Are you having second thoughts? Are you going to back out?"

For the first time, she saw the anxiety in his expression. The consummate diplomat, the gallant leader, was apprehensive. This courageous man, who had been called the Thomas Jefferson of his country and helped to lead Karastonia into the democratic age, was uncertain.

"Yes, I'm having second thoughts, but no, I have no intention of backing out." Her answer lit a flare behind his eyes; her own dropped under the force of his gaze.

"I'm relieved," he said quietly.

"But, Saber, we must reach some kind of accommodation. Aside from the obvious hassle, I can't be comfortable in this situation unless I have your support."

Her words obviously surprised him. "Whatever I can do, Selena. Surely you know that you have my support."

"I know that you are a very busy man, Saber, but do you realize that we've barely spoken to each other? I don't intend to be a distraction..."

He caught her arm and turned her to face him. "Good God, Selena, you're going to be my wife."

"I know. I just wish," she said almost wistfully, "that we knew each other better."

Saber thought he'd never heard such melancholy in a human being's voice before. But he could change her attitude. Once they were married, once they were settled, he'd see that all her qualms were wiped away.

He opened his mouth to assure her that she had no need for regrets, that he wanted—*needed*—for her to be a distraction, that he, too, wanted them to know each other better. But his secretary appeared in the doorway at that moment to tell him there was a call.

"You go on," she urged, resigned. "I think I'll freshen up." She indicated the bath.

His fingers tightened on her elbow and he smiled impatiently, conveying his apology without words.

The guests had begun arriving several days ago. The hotels were filled to overflowing. Karastonia's beautiful coastal resorts rivaled the Riviera and had always been favorite retreats of the jet set and European royalty. Now it seemed that half the continent had flocked to the tiny country on the Aegean. Liners that regularly cruised the Mediterranean added a stop to this summer's itinerary so that the tourists would have a glimpse of the glitterati at play.

The week preceding the wedding seemed to be a nonstop party. Selena and her parents had a large suite in Karastonia's leading hotel. Saber had offered them the hospitality of the palace but she had agreed with her parents that it wouldn't be appropriate until after the wedding.

She had also agreed with her mother, who hadn't wanted to stay with any of her father's numerous relatives. "This is our last chance to be together, just the three of us," Jayne had argued. "Let's spend the time alone with our daughter."

Turnus had finally relented. He'd been somewhat placated that Selena had chosen to have his niece, Alia, as her maid of honor.

For the past two weeks, they had danced and dined and supped and breakfasted. On stage every minute, as she had put it to her cousin. Alia only laughed. She was enjoying herself thoroughly.

Selena always loved visiting her aunts and uncles and cousins on her trips to Karastonia. But this time she also met people who were familiar only from the pages of magazines, newspapers, or on television. And then there were the elaborate wedding gifts—goblets and urns in gold plate, Chinese export porcelain, ancient French tapestries, English antiques—works of art, all of them.

She often asked herself what she was doing here, amidst all this elegant opulence. She was a college instructor, small-town, U.S.A. She couldn't help but speculate about what kinds of things she would have received if she'd been married in Virginia, to, say, another college professor. They would have been inundated by blenders, toasters, sheets, china and crystal, things they would have used every day. But now, nine-tenths of the gifts she and Saber received would surely end up in a museum somewhere.

And the press, the media—always the media—were ever present. After almost two weeks of the nonstop activity, Selena was tired. Turnus was tired. Only Jayne was in her element. And Alia, of course.

On the day before she was to be married, Selena rose early and sought out her father. She stuck her head around the edge of her bedroom door.

He was seated before a tray table, loaded with food. She eyed the abundance. "Good morning. Have you a date for breakfast?" she asked.

"No, thank God," he answered around a bit of kippers. "At least they leave me at peace in the morning."

"Mother?"

"Is still sleeping," he told her. "She needs her rest, although I don't see how she keeps going even with it. Come in, sweetheart."

She took the chair across the table from him, poured herself a cup of coffee and refilled his cup. He thanked her and raised the cup to his lips.

"Daddy, I'm scared."

"Scared, sweetheart?" he asked. "I've never known you to be scared of anything."

She shrugged. "Maybe I shouldn't have said scared. It's really more of a feeling of apprehension over what my life is going to be like."

"This—" He waved a hand to indicate the folderol surrounding the wedding, and Selena had no trouble understanding what he meant. "This is an aberration and will be over as soon as you're safely married. Unfortunately in this day and time, happily married people hold no allure to the press."

"I know," she answered, dismissing that as the problem. "And it's not as though I didn't understand what I was getting into. I could have said no."

At that, her father shifted in his chair and she gave him a questioning look.

"Go on," he said.

Restlessly Selena rose and went to the window. She folded her arms and stood silently, staring at the incredible blue of the sea for several moments. "This is not a romantic relationship. I think you know that. And I don't pretend to believe that romance is necessary for a happy marriage. I had no immediate plans to marry, but I suppose I thought that someday I would find someone I cared about, probably someone in the academic world who shared my interests, someone I wanted to spend the rest of my life with. Then when Saber came... He is so—" she groped for a word "—dynamic. He *handles* things. I'm afraid I won't be able to keep up with him."

"I have no doubt that you will handle things equally well, sweetheart."

She turned back to look at her father. "And then there's the matter of his first wife," she added quietly.

Turnus's reaction was predictable. His face softened into a daydream expression, with a faraway look in his eyes, a small smile on his lips. It was the general effect of her name on everyone who remembered Lisha.

Selena supposed it was natural for people to think of Lisha at a time like this. Selena wasn't sure she remembered the woman at all. She certainly never remembered her having come to the United States with

Saber when he was foreign minister. And though Selena had visited often in Karastonia when she was a youngster, she wasn't sure she'd met Saber's first wife on any of those visits. "From what I understand, she was a paragon. I'm not sure I can live up to that, Daddy."

Turnus turned to her in surprise. "No one expects you to live up to Lisha."

"I'm not sure of that."

"That was a different time, a different world. There was a king on the throne."

"Yes, I know. And I'm not complaining." She smiled. "At least, not much."

She indicated last night's newspaper that was lying on the table in front of the sofa. The editor of the paper had again raised questions about the suitability of an American woman to be the wife of the president. Saber had been furious when he'd seen it.

"You saw the editorial. Saber wants me here to set an example for the women, to encourage them to accept responsibility by taking part in the democratic process. And I can do it, Daddy. I have something to contribute. But I'm afraid that people like that columnist aren't going to take too kindly to my example. He—" again she waved at the paper "—would have preferred Saber marry someone more like his first wife."

"What the editor wants is irrelevant, Selena. It is what Saber wants that is important," her father answered sternly.

"Yes, but it seems I am going to have to walk on eggshells. And you know how good I am at that," she added with a touch of irony. "I tend to say just what I mean."

Turnus laughed. "My dear, you are the daughter of a diplomat. I've been walking on eggshells all my adult life. Besides, you underestimate yourself. I've seen you be charming and gracious to imbeciles on more than one occasion." He grinned.

She came up behind him and wrapped her arms around his neck. Her chuckle joined his laughter. "I love you, you know. I'm going to miss you and Mother."

Turnus patted her arm and they were silent for a minute. Then she leaned around to meet his grin. "And I never appreciated your chutzpah, Daddy. I hope I inherited a bit of that, too. It looks as though I might need it."

"Not at all. Saber will take care of you," said Turnus.

Her father would never understand if she tried to correct his impression so she let the statement lie.

Selena reminded herself of the arrangement with Saber. A year. She would spend a year in Karastonia and if she wasn't content, he would let her go. But that worked both ways.

A year was all he'd promised. If she found that she was indeed happy, it would be up to her to make it more.

Chapter Five

The music from the giant pipe organ—something ponderous by Bach, Selena noticed—was muted by the thick stone walls. She grasped her father's left wrist and looked at his watch. The hands were creeping toward high noon. She gave a nervous smile to her cousin, Alia, her maid of honor and the last of the twelve bridesmaids remaining in the room.

They were all dressed in the same soft shade of pink that lines a conch shell. The flower girls wore ruffled organdy in a deeper shade.

The dark-haired young woman seemed very much at ease.

I wish I were, thought Selena. Numb with apprehension, she waited in the small anteroom near the entrance to the great cathedral and thought of her husband-to-be. Was Nicholas as apprehensive as she was? Was he realizing that now, under the glaring light of all the publicity, it was too late to back out? Was he having regrets?

She looked with distaste at the elaborate bouquet which had just been delivered, and she realized that her hand was hot and clammy.

The bouquet was the one aspect of the wedding that her mother hadn't seen to, and it was much too large even for her fairly tall figure. Perhaps the flowers would have been appropriate if she'd worn the traditional cathedral train.

But, she had decided, and Jayne had concurred, that her life, her duties here, were not to be traditional. And though it was June, and this elaborate wedding would satisfy the most demanding romantic, she was not the traditional twenty-something bride.

So Selena and her mother had decided that sophistication would be more becoming. She had chosen a classic-cut gown of creamy *peau de soie* which was tea length in front and barely brushed the floor in back. The neckline, defined by Brussels lace, was modestly chic. The veil, sewn with tiny stitches to a beaded Juliet cap, would cover her face and shoulders.

"That will not do," said Jayne, tilting her head sideways to study the effect of the bouquet. "Give it to me." Selena surrendered the unwieldy flowers without a word.

A knock on the door signaled the time.

"For God's sake, Jayne," said Turnus, who was visibly nervous. He mopped his brow. "Don't go fooling with that now. We don't have time."

Jayne's clever fingers worked on the flowers but even she was defeated. "This is awful," she moaned.

Suddenly Selena came back to life. She crossed to her mother's side. "Let me." She reached into the center of the bouquet and extracted one distinctive blossom. Called "Path to Heaven," the beautiful flower was to Karastonia what the tulip was to The Netherlands. Similar to the Bird of Paradise, the colors in the stylized flower ranged from azure to indigo and the throat was the same cream as her dress and the small prayerbook she carried. "This will be fine."

She took a deep breath and read her mother's approval in her eyes. "Perfect," said Jayne.

"Well, I guess it's time."

"Be happy, my darling." Her mother kissed her, arranged Selena's veil across her face, nodded satisfaction and disappeared on the arm of an escort.

Alia was next. She gave Selena a hug and left. A moment passed and Selena smiled at her father and tucked her hand into the crook of his elbow. "Shall we go?"

Her father's arm was like steel beneath her fingers. She tried to tell herself that he would support her if she stumbled.

They stepped out of the anteroom. The temperature was several degrees cooler in the cathedral and Selena shivered as she took her first step down that endless aisle. Saber, tall and noteworthy as his build was, seemed a small spot at its end, a small, unfamiliar spot. Her legs would never carry her that far. It was certainly too late for second thoughts, but she had them, anyway.

Oh God, what in the world had she done? She was supposedly an intelligent woman. She must have been insane to agree to such a complicated alliance. She was grateful for the sheer veil that hid her expression from the waiting crowd. A grimace wouldn't be becoming to a bride.

As they approached the halfway point, Nicholas Theodor Saber's form began to increase in size. And continued to grow beyond proportion to their progress, until it filled her vision. His shoulders were impossibly broad. She couldn't see anything else but him.

He was somber in his formal morning coat, his dark eyes unreadable as they met hers. Was he thinking of another woman, another wedding, another day, one swollen with the happy anticipation of young love?

Selena spared only a moment's regret for herself as an adult woman. She had put her romantic fantasies in the drawer with her doctorate years ago. But she was shaken for a brief second, by the loss of the dreams she'd had as an adolescent, dreams she hadn't thought of in years, dreams of everlasting love and happy ever after.

She supposed she should be grateful for the one fairy-tale element in this marriage. There was no question that Saber would have qualified for the handsome prince in anyone's book.

Saber took her hand; her fingers were like ice. Would he notice? Her father stepped back.

The solemn ceremony began. As Saber repeated the vows, his voice was strong and his words, distinct. She mumbled her way through the first passage. Until she realized that to these people, she probably sounded becomingly obsequious. Then she lifted her chin and spoke clearly.

And it was over. Done. She was married—and in the most blatant glare of publicity since the last royal wedding.

Saber raised her veil. He lightly touched his warm lips to hers. The collective gasp that went through the congregation echoed her own. Kissing in public wasn't the norm in Karastonia.

They turned from the altar, the object of all eyes. Her fingers shook as she took his arm.

Saber paused. He covered her shaky fingers with his big hand and looked down at her with a small smile. A flash winked from off to her left. Later, when she saw the photograph of that moment, she would think that they seemed like any couple, dressed in their finery, newly married and deeply in love. The only thing disturbing about the picture was the unexpected possessiveness in Saber's expression.

The day became a tension-filled blur—a formal luncheon followed the ceremony, a public appearance on the balcony of the palace, dancing, champagne toasts, more dancing, a formal dinner. Finally Selena was allowed to escape to change her clothes for the short trip to the yacht.

They were to cruise the Karastonian coast for a ten-day honeymoon.

It was well past midnight when the limousine neared the harbor. Selena noted with some trepidation that the ship was lit up like a Christmas tree. She glanced at her new husband, hoping there were no further formalities to be endured.

Saber had changed into a dark suit and she was wearing a dress that would have been appropriate for another formal party. However, she could see no press, no cameras, and she gave a sigh of relief.

Saber heard. He smiled. "Tired?"

"A little bit," she admitted. "You, on the other hand, look as fresh as a daisy."

"Appearances are deceiving, but I'm all right." He scraped his hand down his face and she could see that he was indeed weary.

"I don't suppose it was easy for you to clear your calendar for ten days."

He didn't deny it; he simply shrugged.

She looked down at her lap. "Now, you make me feel a bit guilty."

He was surprised. "Why should you feel guilty?"

"Because all I've had to do is attend parties. You've had to attend the parties and do double work, as well. When did you sleep, Saber?"

He gave a dry laugh. "I'm fortunate to be one of those people who doesn't require a lot of sleep."

The captain was waiting to greet them at the quay. She acknowledged the man's good wishes as he gave them both a smart salute and helped her aboard the tender. "Welcome, sir, ma'am."

"Thank you." Selena smiled as enthusiastically as possible under the circumstances. She was almost asleep on her feet. She swallowed a yawn as she followed the captain's directions to a cushioned seat under a small awning.

Saber sat very close to her; she had to fight the temptation to rest her tired head on his shoulder. He seemed to sense her need and laid a strong, supportive arm across her shoulders and pulled her close.

Selena tilted her head back to give him a grateful smile. She wondered immediately if his show of affection was for the benefit of the captain.

She chided herself. She knew she shouldn't look for a hidden motive behind every move he made, but she couldn't help it.

From the first, the media had played up their wedding as a romantic union of two people in love. Once, Saber had talked to her about the portrayal.

"I hope showing a small amount of public affection doesn't make you uncomfortable, Selena," he'd said as they were leaving a party hand in hand.

"Of course not," she had responded without perceptible hesitation. Not *un*comfortable, exactly. But not yet comfortable, either, she had told herself honestly.

Still, she relaxed under the weight of Saber's arm. It was a short, quiet trip out to the yacht. As soon as they reached the vessel, however, the tension returned.

Saber took her hand as they mounted the ladder to the deck. He seemed to sense her exhaustion, though she was sure she'd managed to hide the worst of it, because he cut short the crew's greetings and, still holding her hand, escorted her down a short flight of steps and forward. He opened the door to the salon of the master suite and indicated one of the bedrooms opening off from it.

"That is your stateroom," he said, leading her toward the open door. He released her hand, tugged at his tie and opened the top button of his shirt.

She looked through the door into the spacious cabin, where someone obviously had unpacked her things. Her silver-backed brush and comb were on the dressing table. The bed had been turned back and the sheer white gown and peignoir her mother had selected in New York were arranged across it. New York seemed like another lifetime, on another planet. She realized that Saber was staring at the flimsy lingerie. Her color rose.

"I'm right over there," he added, gesturing toward a door on the opposite side of the salon. His smile was slightly twisted. "I'll leave you now, Selena. Get a good night's sleep. Call if you need anything." She felt his lips on her forehead.

Though she was exhausted, she was also oddly, unexplainably disappointed by his hurried, almost hasty, good-night. This was, after all, the first night of their marriage. It would seem more fitting to relax together in the salon for a minute's conversation. She opened her mouth to suggest something of the kind.

Saber waited politely.

Finally, however, she simply nodded. "You're right. We probably both need rest. Good night, Saber."

The door closed behind him. She looked at the gown, made a face and stripped off her dress. In the drawer she found a few things that must have raised the eyebrows of whomever unpacked her clothes. She dragged her favorite old Redskins football jersey over her head and crawled beneath the covers.

Married. She reached for a pillow and brought it to her chest. She looked down at her hand, at the shining gold band that proclaimed the actuality.

The diamond-and-ruby engagement ring had been shifted to her right hand for the ceremony. Now she pulled it off and placed it in a dish on the bedside table. But she left the wedding ring in place.

Married... to a man she barely knew.

Saber peeled off his jacket and tossed it on his own bed. He rolled his sleeves back, whipped off his tie and slung it away with an impatient gesture. He opened another button of his shirt. Then he returned to the sitting room and collapsed into a chair.

Hell! What had he done?

As he had stood at the altar this morning, waiting for his bride, he had suddenly been hit with the strangest feeling. He'd let his eyes roam over the congregation, looking around at his friends, personal, political and professional. He'd been shocked as he realized the power represented by many of the people in the cathedral, powerful people assembled from all over the world.

And, suddenly, Saber had longed to be anywhere but where he was.

Later, at the reception, as he'd shaken hands, smiled and introduced Selena, he'd tried, on another level of his mind, to make excuses for the urge, to tell himself that he was simply tired. All the worn-out clichés had come too easily to mind. The excitement of having been in on the birth of a nation was waning. The burdens of his position were heavy. The rewards were no longer enough; the pressure of his job was finally reaching him.

But Saber had known this morning that this time it was more than a clichéd reaction to pressure. He had recognized, for the first time, that he had never had a life of his own.

He'd been groomed for important work from the time he was a child. His parents, although not warm people, had been considerate enough and not overtly demanding. They had merely assumed that he would do what was expected of him. And he had never disappointed them. But now, suddenly, he wished his existence were easier, tamer, more normal.

The entire concept of wanting more time for a personal life for himself had jolted him anew as he'd stood in the receiving line at the reception, but he'd realized it was true. Now, here in the salon of the master's cabin, he finally located the privacy, quiet and solitude he needed to reexamine the prospect and his attitude toward it.

He, Nicholas Saber, fancied the opportunity for leisure. Now that the situation in the country had begun to stabilize, he could delegate more authority. He mulled over ways that could be accomplished. Not right away, of course. He'd been elected; he had to serve out his term.

As he stared out over the sea he laughed aloud, the sound emerging as a dry and disillusioned bark. Here he sat, thinking he'd like to simplify his life, and he had just landed himself with another complication, perhaps the most complex, the largest complication of all.

A wife... a wife whom he barely knew.

As is often the case when exhaustion sets in, Selena's mind refused to release its grip on consciousness. She lay there wide-eyed for half an hour, listening to the motors, feeling the gentle rocking motion of the

She made an ineffectual motion with her hand and stepped into the room. "I couldn't sleep. Too keyed up, I expect."

"Would you like something? A brandy?" He held up his glass, the bowl resting in his large palm.

His gaze had drifted to her bare legs. She should go back into the bedroom and close the door. She hesitated, thinking of the expression of loneliness and regret that she'd caught on his face.

Was he thinking of his dead wife? Was he remembering the love they'd shared, the marriage that was so very different from this one?

Suddenly Selena decided to set aside her own misgivings and try to do something for this man who was her husband. She'd figuratively made her bed. Mistake or not, it was up to her to find a way to be comfortable in it. And she certainly wouldn't find comfort if he didn't find it, as well.

A tiny smile played at one corner of her mouth. "What I'd really like is something to eat."

He laughed as he got to his feet. "I can take care of that easily enough." He went to the desk and picked up the telephone.

"Saber, no. It's too late," she protested, coming farther into the room.

"If my bride is hungry, it is never too late. How about a cheeseburger and a soda?"

He'd obviously been talking to her mother. She loved junk food. "A cheeseburger sounds wonderful, but I'll soon be spoiled by such indulgence."

He looked at her for a minute, seemingly trying to decide something. She stood still under his examination. At last he smiled. "I doubt seriously that a little indulgence would spoil you."

She studied him, puzzled by the remark. "What do you mean by that?"

He shrugged and sipped from his brandy. "I was sitting here feeling guilty."

"Why on earth would you feel guilty?"

"I've asked a lot of you. I suppose I've just now stopped to think how much. I feel guilty about what you've given up."

So that was the reason for his expression—or at least a partial reason. She thought for a minute. What could she say?

"You're giving up a lot, too, Saber," she said lightly. "I intend to be a very demanding wife."

He lifted a dark brow. A corner of his mouth twitched. "Do you now?"

Selena relaxed. "I want mustard, catsup *and* mayonnaise on my cheeseburger. I like it rare, with tomato on the side."

Saber laughed as he went to the telephone and ordered for both of them. Burgers, fries, soft drinks.

"I'll get some clothes on," she said.

He started to say something, then changed his mind and nodded.

Back in the bedroom Selena looked at the lovely silk lingerie set that she'd tossed over a chair. She dismissed it as too suggestive. She pulled on a pair of white pants and socks and caught her hair back in a clasp.

"It will be here soon," he told her when she returned to the sitting room. "With tomato on the side. Our wedding supper was wasted on us both, it seems."

She knew he was teasing. "Wedding supper" was a misnomer, to say the least. The guests had been served from an elaborate banquet table that groaned under the weight of the food. Still, she answered seriously. "I was too nervous to eat anything."

"Right now a cheeseburger is probably more appropriate fare to accompany the sort of talk we need to have, anyway."

The comment drew her eyes to his face. He wasn't looking at her.

"Talk?" she asked mildly. She wanted to comfort him, she wanted to feel relaxed in his company, but she wasn't sure she was up to a serious talk. Not tonight.

"I know you're troubled, Selena. About your changed status, about what your life will be like. God, after the past few weeks, I am a bit uneasy, myself."

"You are?" Even having witnessed his sad expression, his choice of words surprised her.

"Certainly. Everything has happened too rapidly for either of us to have adjusted. We knew it will take some time. That's why I promised you that we wouldn't share a bedroom until you decided the time was right."

If she ever did, thought Selena. Still, it was kind of him to restate the conditions of their marriage. Reassuring, somehow. Especially in light of the way he'd looked at her legs when she entered the room.

She began to relax. The numbness faded and was replaced, not by depression as she'd feared, but by a growing curiosity about this man she'd married. Her thoughts were interrupted by a knock on the door.

A young man in uniform came in bearing a huge tray, which he set on the table in front of Selena. If he was surprised by her casual attire he was much too well-trained to let on.

Her eyes widened at the amount of food. "Good grief, Saber. Are we supposed to eat all this?"

The young man blushed and cleared his throat. "The chef thought you might like a choice of his desserts. Something sweet to finish with. Er…" His voice trailed off and the color in his face turned a screaming red. "He's famous for his sweets."

Selena caught her breath.

Saber nodded, unsmiling. "Thank you. That will be all."

The young man beat a hasty retreat.

The door had barely closed behind him when Saber burst out laughing. It was a relaxed, happy sound.

Selena tried to hide her surprise. Was this the same man whose loneliness was etched on his face a few minutes ago? The mask of dignity he habitually wore seemed to have been cast aside. He looked years younger.

His laughter died, but a smile lingered around the curve of his mouth. "I think he was baffled by your football shirt. He's probably never seen one before. I wonder what he thinks the number designates."

She looked down at her chest. The numerals 20 were painted there. "My age?" A grin began to grow as other possibilities occurred to her.

His mind must have been running along the same lines because he grinned, too. "Do you think the chef wanted to provide us with something to keep our energy level high?" he asked, chuckling as he eyed the elaborate selection.

Her gaze followed his. "If so, he certainly is optimistic," she said.

There was what her mother would have called a "pregnant pause," followed by a moment of silence, but then Saber laughed again.

She joined in his laughter, grateful that the atmosphere between them was the easiest it had ever been. Perhaps...

Selena wondered if the reporters, who wrote so romantically of their marriage, would have believed that they spent their wedding night, what was left of it, munching on cheeseburgers, French fries and Grand Marnier soufflé, and talking about American football.

Chapter Six

Selena woke on the softest, smoothest sheets she'd ever slept upon. She stretched, paused and looked around in confusion. Yes, this was her bedroom; there was her purse on the dressing table.

But she was unable to remember how she got here. She remembered yawning a lot; she remembered her eyelids growing heavy. The last thing she remembered was asking Saber to pour her a cup of coffee. She needed a jolt of caffeine to keep herself awake.

She turned her head warily and then closed her eyes with a soft sigh. She was sure that she still wore her slacks at that point, but this morning they were folded neatly on the same chair where she'd discarded the sheer gown and peignoir. Warmth crept into her cheeks. Well, they *were* married.

She bathed and pulled on her swimsuit, a new one selected by her mother. She observed herself dubiously in the floor-length mirror of the bathroom, then rolled her eyes. It was midnight blue, a sleek wet-look fabric, and it zipped up the front. At the top of the zipper there was a large ring. The legs of the suit were cut very high on her thighs. Too high, in her opinion.

Why had she ever let Jayne take care of this purchase alone? Or any other, for that matter, she thought, her eyes sliding to the extravagant lingerie that she'd passed up last night.

She turned her body to look at herself, this time from the rear. The sight caused a soft moan to escape from her lips. Her mother had obviously decided that a certificate of marriage and a ring upon one's finger necessitated a bathing garment that was blatantly seductive. She picked up a knee-length robe and hurriedly slipped her arms into the sleeves.

Heaven knows what else I'll find when I finish unpacking, she thought as she left the suite and went looking for Saber.

He was in the main salon immersed in reports. But as soon as she entered, he dropped what he was doing and rose.

Her heart took a plunge when she saw that his mask of dignity was once again firmly in place. But he smiled as he came to her side and took her in his arms. His lips were cool and he seemed to be holding himself in check. She reminded herself, as he kissed her, that the affection was for the benefit of the crew.

However, a moment later she wondered if the kiss needed to be quite so thorough. His cool lips were suddenly warm and hungry and firm against hers. When he finally raised his head she was slightly breathless. While he appeared to be totally in control of himself she did notice a muscle contract in his strong jaw.

"Did you sleep well?" he asked, still holding her. His breath caressed her cheek as he studied her face.

Her voice was calm but her eyes flickered as she answered, "What little sleep I had was very restful, thank you."

That appealing masculine slash appeared in his cheek, but it was gone in a fleeting moment. "Would you like some breakfast?"

She pulled out of his arms. "Surely you're kidding, Saber. After last night I may not eat again for a week." Despite their amusement at the chef's selection of sweets, they had managed to put quite a dent in the assortment.

"If you are going to be busy," she went on, noticing the scattered papers, "I might work on my tan."

"I do have a few things that have to be attended to. All the problems don't stop when the president takes a honeymoon. I'll join you as soon as I can."

"Don't rush. I understand."

She left him there and made her way to the forward sun deck that she'd seen from their quarters. It was guaranteed privacy from the rest of the ship by a screen. She took off her robe and lay down on a padded chaise lounge. In moments she was asleep again.

Saber found her there half an hour later. He looked at her for a full minute, letting his unguarded gaze roam over her long, smooth legs, her small waist and full breasts. The ring at the top of her suit was a formidable temptation. He never would have believed that this woman he'd married could be so sensuous, so unconsciously seductive. But the last weeks had been arduous and trying, and not because of all the work he had to do. He shook his head. She was completely unaware of how quickly his desire for her was growing.

Last night he'd been surprised by something he'd not thought likely—that he could relax with her, that they would converse as friends and companions. Later, though, when he'd carried her to bed, when he'd unsnapped and unzipped her white slacks and peeled them off her, he'd been hard-pressed—he laughed at the very appropriate expression—not to kiss and caress her into arousal.

He'd known she was lovely. He'd known that, eventually, making love to her would be a pleasure. But he'd not expected any difficulty about waiting until they had learned some things about each other. He'd not expected to be in this uncomfortable and constant state of near-arousal when he was near her.

It was a dilemma, one that she'd soon notice since they were going to be together in close quarters for ten days. His new wife wasn't blind.

This morning he found half of himself wishing for a state emergency that would necessitate their returning to the capital. But the other half wanted to take her to his bed and sail on endlessly while he lost himself in her sensuality.

Suddenly annoyed, Saber spun away from the sight. He returned to the main salon and picked up the papers he'd been working on earlier. Luckily for his peace of mind, there was always business to be taken care of.

Selena heard her stomach growl before she realized she was hungry. She picked up her watch from the table beside the lounge. She'd been here for over an hour. This early in the season, she had very little tan and had to be careful not to burn. She got to her feet and put on her robe. Then she went looking for Saber.

She found him conferring with the captain in the main salon. He turned when she entered. "I thought we might have dinner tonight in Entchulla. What do you think?" he asked her.

She recognized the name of the small harbor town fifty or sixty miles down the coast from the capital.

"Sure." She smiled and drew closer. He held out his arm in invitation and she had no hesitation about moving easily into the embrace. "I think that sounds wonderful. I haven't been there in years but I seem to remember a little Italian restaurant near the harbor."

"Indeed, it is still there." He seemed pleased that she was familiar with the town. "That's where I planned for us to eat tonight."

The captain spoke again. "Very well, sir. We should dock about seven o'clock," he said. Then he left them alone.

Saber instantly and abruptly dropped his arm.

Before he could go back to his papers, Selena made some offhand remark to cover her shock—she wasn't sure afterward what she'd said.

Saber's response was unexpectedly stilted and withdrawn. To say his attitude surprised her would be an understatement. Last night they had talked easily and openly, as though they were friends—or at least, headed in that direction.

She looked up at her husband with clouded eyes but he didn't meet her gaze. She wondered what had happened between last night and today. She had never been one to skip around an issue so she asked, "Saber, is something wrong?"

"What do you think is wrong?" he asked, now introducing a strong cord of irony into the conversation. He sighed heavily—as though she were a pesky problem he had to deal with before he could get on with more important things—and touched her arm in apparent apology. "Nothing's wrong, Selena. We both knew the first few weeks were going to be difficult," he added with more sincerity. "We just have to wade through them. Besides, the business of state never really stops." He indicated the papers on his desk with a wave of his arm. "I have to finish these before the day is over."

She withdrew a step, provoking a narrowed look. "I'll leave you to it, then," she said stiffly. Then she announced, "I'm going to find some lunch. Will you join me or shall I have the chef send you a tray?"

"A tray, please," he answered absently, returning his attention to the papers in front of him.

Selena had to make a real effort not to stomp out. She couldn't believe it. The kiss he'd given her this morning had left her shaken. The first full day of their marriage and her new husband could kiss her eagerly in front of others; but when they didn't have an audience, he became so engrossed in his work that he couldn't spare the time to have lunch alone with her.

For a long minute, Saber watched the doorway through which she had disappeared, a guarded expression in his black eyes.

* * *

They met for drinks together that evening before the trip to Entchulla. Saber served Selena, then sat down beside her on the plush sofa.

After only a few minutes, however, even that brief interlude of privacy was interrupted by a call.

When Saber came back from the radio room he was all business again. "Do you have any objections if one of the appointments secretaries begins to set up a schedule for you?" he asked. "There have been quite a few requests coming in to the office for you to appear at various functions."

"I don't mind. Will I have to give a speech? I would need time to prepare for that."

He shook his head. "You could get by with saying a few words of thanks or encouragement, depending on the circumstances. I'll tell the secretary to limit the appearances to ceremonial occasions for now, until they can consult with you."

"Fine," she said, and he left her to return to the radio room.

She sensed that she was being handled like a commodity, but then scolded herself for the feeling. She'd known she would be expected to do this sort of thing. What Saber hadn't told her before their marriage about her duties as wife of the president, her father had filled in.

The villagers had seen the yacht offshore and were waiting when the tender docked. The newlyweds were welcomed warmly and briefly, and then left to enjoy their meal. Again, Selena was aware of Saber's withdrawal once they were alone.

* * *

Determined to discuss the situation between them, which could easily take on a nightmarish quality, Selena rose early on the second full day of the trip—she refused to call it a honeymoon, even to herself—and donned a floor-length terry-cloth robe she'd gotten last Christmas. She didn't want to take the time to dress because she might miss Saber when he left his room.

She was waiting in the salon that separated their bedrooms. "Good morning, Saber," she said, turning from the window when he entered.

"Good morning," he answered, a surprised smile smoothing out his features.

"I would like to talk to you," she said, her tone businesslike. She thought he took an instinctive step in her direction, but only one. When she looked at him expectantly, he halted.

"Certainly," he answered, recovering quickly. "Shall we go out on deck for breakfast? We can talk there."

"No." She spread her arms. "As you can see I'm not dressed yet."

"We were out late. I thought you would still be in bed."

She dropped her arms and pushed her hands into the pockets of the robe. "I wanted to catch you before you went to work." She hesitated. "You were going to work, weren't you?"

He nodded shortly.

"I thought this was to be a time for us to get to know each other, Saber."

"And I thought you realized—"

"I do," she interrupted. "I do realize that the government doesn't ever stop. I am not going to be a demanding wife, or a complaining one. But yesterday's off-again, on-again show of affection made me edgy." Irritated was what it made her, but she chose the other word as more diplomatic.

He gave her a long, hard look. She knew she'd surprised him again; she just wasn't sure whether the surprise was because she dared to speak honestly or because she dared to criticize him.

"I apologize if I made you uncomfortable," he said with no expression in his voice.

"I think you should tone down the public display. I know a certain amount of affection between us is expected, and I'm willing to go along, but you aren't being consistent. You give me a rather enthusiastic kiss one minute, and the next you're poring over papers as though I don't even exist."

When he didn't answer immediately, she went on, "We promised to be honest with each other, Saber, and that's what I'm trying to do."

"Very well," he answered simply. "I'll see you on deck for breakfast?" He waited for her nod of agreement before leaving.

After he'd gone, Selena stood staring at the door. How could the man maintain such control?

The initial result of Selena's straightforward discussion with Saber was that the relationship between them now became like a silly children's game. She became the one to withdraw and was particularly adept at avoiding his displays of affection. She didn't think she was making an issue of her withdrawal—the first time it happened, he looked at her with a brow lifted in question. She simply smiled. But after one or two more foiled attempts, he clearly realized what she was doing.

He didn't press her. However, he did begin to spend more time with her. They swam and fished from the stern. Selena caught a large albacore, albeit with Saber's help. They dined on deck under the stars, or on shore in one of the many quaint villages that dotted the coast. They danced to the stereo on board and to the music of either a concertina or a guitar in the villages. But they didn't dance too closely.

She beat him at Scrabble; he beat her at chess.

And there was no way to completely avoid the accidental physical contact, which was beginning to affect her profoundly despite her misgivings.

With each touch, no matter how casual, she felt her desire grow. She often caught his dark gaze upon her, and it had its result, sparking a surprising need. She felt the warm surge of desire more than once under the force of that gaze.

They also argued, sometimes with amusement, sometimes with annoyance. Many of their problems were the result of cultural differences; there was no getting around that. No matter how broad-minded he professed to be, he occasionally lapsed into the dominating male role that was so common to his countrymen.

Underneath it all, under the casual laughter and occasional discord, it was obvious to Selena, and, she thought, to Saber, that the tension between them was building relentlessly. Their efforts at control were eroding, slowly but invariably, like layer after layer of sand washed from the beach by a gentle tide.

Whether the situation would either explode into full-blown anger or flaming passion was a question yet to be decided. . . .

Selena rose early, determined to maintain a positive mood today. They were leaving the ship to visit the ruin of a remote hilltop temple constructed centuries ago by their Greek ancestors.

It was a short climb to the site, so she dressed appropriately in dark blue shorts and a cool cotton shirt in a lighter shade of the same color. She twisted her hair into one long braid, picked up a canvas tote and left the stateroom to join Saber on deck for a hasty breakfast.

When she appeared, he stood politely and she took her seat opposite him. He remained standing for a minute looking down at her, his napkin dangling from his hand. He was different today, somehow, she thought as she observed the play of muscle across his broad shoulders. More relaxed.

He was dressed as casually as she. His shorts and shirt were khaki. His long muscular legs and forearms were tanned a beautiful bronze color and lightly dusted with hair. He looked very. . . macho.

And there was an odd light in his eye. She laughed uncomfortably under the intensity of his stare. "Something wrong?" She touched her nose, her hair, raised her brows inquiringly.

"No, of course not," he said quickly.

The sun was blindingly bright in the cloudless sky. She squinted in the harsh light, fitted a white tennis visor on her head and reached for a glass of juice.

When they had finished eating, Saber went to have a final word with the captain.

Selena watched him go. The sun's effect was responsible for the warmth she was feeling, for her accelerated pulse rate. At least, that's what she told herself.

She wandered over to rest her forearms on the rail and looked out at the beach that was their destination. From here it looked beautiful, but desolate. A few gulls, some breeze-swept grasses and the flow of gentle waves as they greeted the shore, contributed the only motion in the scene. The mountain looked larger than she'd expected; she had a clear view of the ruined temple at the top and it seemed very far away.

"The tender is waiting," Saber said from behind her, startling her.

"I'm ready," she answered with a smile, holding up her tote bag. He led the way down the ladder to the smaller boat and turned back to give her a hand. She hopped in and headed for the cushioned seat in the bow.

When Saber joined her a moment later, he was barefoot and carrying a pair of low-topped hiking boots with socks stuffed down inside. "I hope my sneakers will be okay, Saber. I don't have any boots."

He nodded, his gaze moving leisurely down her bare legs to her feet. "Sneakers are fine. It's not much of a climb. But you'd better take them off for now, if you don't want to get them wet. We'll have to wade ashore."

Selena nodded and removed the sneakers and her socks and stuffed them into the tote bag. The sailor maneuvered the tender as close to the beach as possible.

Saber balanced on one hand and jumped with effortless grace over the gunwale, barely creating a splash. Before Selena could join him in the water, she felt his hands firmly about her waist.

To her surprise he lifted her easily. Her hands went to his shoulders for balance, to the steel-hard muscles under his shirt, while her eyes sought his questioningly. It was such a playfully intimate thing to do, to lift her like this. And so unlike the Nicholas Saber she was learning to know.

His face was in shadow but his beautiful dark eyes met hers, met and held. He set her on her feet in water that was knee-deep, and held her until she steadied. He removed his hands slowly, almost—it seemed—reluctantly. "Go on in. I'll get our things."

What was going on here? She finally dragged her gaze from his and waded up the slight slope toward the deserted beach.

Saber reached back in the boat. He grabbed his own boots and gathered up a couple of towels and the picnic lunch, which had been prepared by the chef and packed in a knapsack. "Come back for us late this afternoon," he called out to the young man.

"Yes, sir." He saluted and revved the engine. The tender swung about in a long, smooth arc while Saber joined Selena on the beach.

Side by side, they stood watching the wake of the small boat until it disappeared.

When the sound of the motor had faded away, Selena turned to look around the area. "This is nice," she said softly. "Peaceful."

Saber had been here before so he watched her instead. He smiled to himself; her delight was unmistakable.

On the crest of the hill high above them was the outline of the ruins they would explore. But there were no other houses or buildings of any kind, no power lines, no other evidence that man had ever left a footprint on this spot.

He moved toward her until he could smell her scent, that fresh clean smell that was so much a part of her. The breeze from the sea lifted strands of hair off her neck. "Do you realize that this is the first time we've ever been completely alone?" he asked in a husky voice.

Selena had not been unaware of Saber's nearness. Slowly she turned to him. Now the wind and sun were at her back. His expression was the one that was exposed and the open desire she saw in his eyes sent her heart up to lodge in her throat.

Not that she hadn't been expecting something of the sort, a heated look here, a touch there—the warnings were evident. But now, today, it seemed the tension had clearly reached the unbearable point.

"I hadn't thought about it." She lied, trying to ignore the effect of their isolation and the sight of his powerful body.

The khaki shirt was buttoned carelessly, and the thick, dark hair curling damply on his chest, as well as an irregular pulsebeat under the skin of his throat, were a temptation to her fingers. She wanted to touch him intimately and the fact swooped down on her so unexpectedly that she caught her breath at its force. She raised her eyes to his.

Suddenly Saber dropped the things he was carrying and reached out for her. He didn't ask permission, didn't stop to think that this might be a foolish move, didn't think he might regret the action. He simply surrendered to an urge that was so strong, so primitive, that it would no longer be denied. He'd barely slept since they left the capital, knowing that a few feet away his wife lay in a large bed clad only in a football jersey, her long legs bare.

He hadn't made love to a woman since the night he had proposed to Selena.

With his big capable hands he brought her soft curves into alignment with the sharper planes of his body. God—he almost groaned aloud—she felt good against him. And, bless the powers above, she tilted her head back, laid her hands on his chest and rose up on tiptoe.

The glorious sun rode the clear blue sky above their heads. He looked down into her face. The crystal radiance clarified each of her fine features and painted the flawless purity of her skin a golden color. He could feel the heat on his shoulders, smell its warmth in her hair and on her skin. "You are so beautiful," he murmured.

A sigh escaped; his mouth sought hers hungrily, and he could taste the simmering flavor of sunlight on her soft lips. He flicked her lips with his tongue and she opened her mouth to his exploration. Her teeth were slick; she tasted early morning fresh and minty and sweet, so sweet.

When he finally lifted his head they were both breathing rapidly. Deliberately, holding her dreamy gaze with his, he slid his hands down her back to her hips and held her close, trying to ease the ache in him. "I want you, Selena."

Her eyes widened as she felt the evidence of his arousal. "Saber—" she said hesitantly.

"I know, I'm out of line," he declared harshly. A muscle in his jaw convulsed. "But, you wanted honesty. Dear God, I didn't realize that I would want to make love to you quite so quickly, and so desperately. I won't force you, but I'm hurting, Selena. And we are married."

She let her head fall forward until her forehead rested on his chest. "Oh, Saber." She shook her head. When she raised her eyes to his again, she wore a small smile. "I won't pretend I haven't felt this coming on. You could probably convince me."

She saw the satisfaction flare in his eyes.

"But I'm not certain this would not be wise. Not yet."

The satisfaction didn't fade as she'd expected it to. "Why would it not be wise?" he asked with an indulgent smile that was hard to resist.

She touched his cheek; the muscle jerked again. She pulled free, surprised at how agonizing the action was. "For a lot of reasons," she answered evenly. "We promised ourselves we would get to know each other. You just said it yourself, Saber. This is the first time we've even been completely alone. What if we make a mistake?"

Saber shoved his hands into his pockets and nodded shortly. His eyes were black and hot as they roamed over her. "And you are nervous. Why, Selena?"

She hesitated, wondering about the best way to tell him. It was something he would discover eventually. It was better for him to know what to expect, and they had pledged to be honest. "I haven't had a lot of experience at this kind of thing."

The silence with which he greeted her words was deafening. But the rhythmic pounding of the ocean rushed in to fill the void. She risked a look.

Saber was clearly stunned by her revelation. When he finally spoke, the words were delivered as an accusation. "Are you trying to tell me that you're a virgin?" he demanded, his voice rising on the last word.

"I'm not *trying* to tell you anything. I *am* telling you—I am not sexually experienced." She couldn't imagine why he should be angry about such a thing. What difference could it make to him? It was her business. "I'm sorry if it bothers you."

But he was angry. His brows met above his eyes, his lips thinned, his fingers curved into his palms. He was very angry.

As though she had betrayed him.

"I suppose now you'll expect me to set a romantic scene when we do go to bed together."

She paused; the moment stretched into eternity. "You?" she responded finally with a smile saturated in disdain. "Certainly not." Her anger rose to meet his. She lifted her chin to a "go-to-hell" angle. She spun on her heel and started to walk away from him. "But the choices I've made about my life have not really been your concern, have they?" She tossed the parting shot over her shoulder.

"Until now," he returned sharply. Hands thrust into his pockets, he followed her. "Why the devil didn't you tell me?"

"I didn't realize that such experience was part of your job description," she answered without turning.

The sandy white beach blurred before her eyes, but she kept her head up and kept on walking. She had gone a hundred feet or more before he spoke again from behind her.

"Selena—" From his tone of voice he appeared to have gained control of himself.

But Selena was not appeased. How dare he take that insulting, accusatory tone with her? As though what she had were contagious.

Determinedly, she continued her chosen path parallel to the waterline. A random breeze pulled at the tennis visor she wore and she tugged it back down into place.

"Selena," he persisted. "Where are you going?"

"Anywhere, nowhere," she snapped. "Away from you." She tossed her braid over her shoulder and lengthened her stride.

At last, with a firm hand on her arm, he brought her to a halt.

She gave his hand a pointed look.

He dropped it immediately. "Stop it. You can't run away forever. I'm sorry I overreacted, but it was a shock. You'll have to admit that finding out that you are a virgin—"

"Because I'm over thirty? Or maybe because I'm an American?"

"Neither. That wasn't what I meant at all." He plunged the fingers of one hand through his hair in a gesture of frustration. Or was it exasperation? "I really do apologize, Selena. I didn't mean to insult you," he assured her quietly.

"You didn't," she retorted promptly and with determination. When he looked disbelieving, she went on, "But you have disappointed me, Saber. The first night of our marriage I thought that perhaps we would be able to come to terms with each other fairly quickly."

Back in Virginia, she had allowed that passion-heady love wasn't the best basis for marriage because it seldom lasted. On the other hand, she did want them to feel *something* for each other. "I didn't expect romance, but I guess I did expect consistency. Instead, the next morning you were like a different man completely. It was as though the man who had eaten cheeseburgers with me had never existed."

Saber took a deep breath, stretching the cotton shirt across his broad chest. He planted his hands on his hips and glared down at her. "Do you want to know what happened?" he snapped.

His height, his broad shoulders made her feel diminutive in comparison, and she was far from being either dainty or petite. She realized that, despite his stance, his anger was no longer directed at her, but directed inwardly toward himself. "Yes."

"Because, the next morning I came to the pool and watched while you sunbathed. You remember that bathing suit—ah, yes, I can see from your expression that you do. The wet-suit look, I think they call it, complete with a zipper down the front. I realized then that it was going to be difficult—in fact, it was going to be damned near impossible—to keep my hands off of you when we were alone."

He ignored her gasp of astonishment. "No comment?" he asked after a minute. "Oh, hell, Selena, come on. Let's climb a mountain. Maybe if we work off some of this energy it will be easier."

They didn't speak while they sat in the sand and donned their shoes and socks. Saber slung the knapsack on his back and they set off.

The mountain wasn't brutal, but it wasn't easy, either. Saber led the way but kept an eye on her until he was satisfied that she wasn't a bumblefoot. They stopped to rest once on an outcropping of rock that was about two-thirds of the way to the summit.

Saber leaned down to give her a hand. He grasped her forearm and effortlessly boosted her up beside him. "Ah, thanks," she said, taking a moment to catch her breath. "I must be out of shape."

"I wouldn't say that," he murmured, his gaze lingering on her damp shirt.

She let the provocative remark pass. She did feel calmer for the exercise. She hadn't really done anything strenuous, hadn't played tennis or swum, since—good heavens—since the weekend Saber had proposed. No wonder she was keyed up.

They climbed until they had nearly reached the summit. "Look," said Saber, dropping their equipment and turning her until her back was to him. His hands remained on her shoulders. "It will rain later."

She felt the warm weight of his fingers as she looked toward the water. Except for the sound of the wind, it was quiet. A few dark clouds, touched at the edges with silver, had moved out over the blue waters.

Through gaps in the clouds, sunbeams radiated down like dozens of golden pillars holding up the sky.

"Oh, Saber," she murmured. "I've never seen anything so beautiful and dramatic." She looked over her shoulder to meet his smiling eyes.

And could not look away.

Suddenly the tension was back, vibrating between their locked gazes like a strummed wire. The resonance reached all the way to her toes. He moved his hands down her arms to her hands. Linking their fingers, he wrapped both of their arms across her stomach and pulled her against his broad chest. She saw his eyes darken, became aware of the acceleration of his heartbeat against her back. She felt her knees weaken and was sublimely grateful for the support of his body.

Saber dipped his head with the obvious intention of kissing her. But, at the last second, when their lips were only millimeters apart, he stopped. His mouth curved in a small smile that unnerved her. "Ah, Selena. What am I going to do with you?"

His tone was low and seemed to have grown dangerously mellow, but she had no trouble understanding him. However, she couldn't have spoken if her life had depended on it. She shook her head.

"Shall we see if we can reach the top?" He grinned wryly. "Of the mountain," he added smoothly.

She nodded.

"The rest of the climb isn't as difficult as it has been so far."

Clearly he was speaking metaphorically and she felt her pulse accelerate. She finally found her voice. "Yes, I understand."

He hugged her quickly and let her go. "Come on. I'm hungry."

Half an hour later they unfolded the cloth on the steps of the ruined temple and unpacked the food. "This looks delicious," said Selena, spreading a napkin across her lap. She filled a plate for each of them with fresh crudités, dried fruits, bits of smoked meat and sharp cheeses and fresh-baked bread.

Saber poured a rich red wine into two plastic cups and handed one to her. He touched his cup to hers. "To a beautiful day spent with a beautiful woman," he said, his voice dropping to a low, intimate level.

"Thank you," she responded.

Most of the clouds had moved out to sea and the temple ruins were once again splotched with sunlight. Saber smiled at her, and after a moment they both turned their attention to the food. A tenuous peace hung between them as the afternoon melted away. That, for the time being, was enough.

The same smile was in place on Saber's face early that evening while he waited for Selena to join him in the main salon. The promise of the afternoon clouds had been fulfilled and a cool rain was falling, streaking the windows. The stereo played softly in the background and candlelight cast deep, curious shadows into the corners of the room.

A small table had been set for two before the window. He looked around, wondering if she would be uncomfortable in the blatantly seductive scene.

He shrugged as he checked his formal bow tie in the reflection from the silver ice cooler. After today, surely they were past that. His wife wanted him. And he sure as hell wanted her. They'd both recognized and admitted the sensual attraction. Now, the decision made, he was merely trying to speed up the timetable.

As surprised as he'd been when she made her announcement this morning, he found that he was beginning to get used to the idea of an inexperienced wife. His initial shock had been for her sake, because she deserved more than this "arranged" marriage he'd foisted on her...and for his sake, because he had expected a worldly sophisticate to whom the physical aspects of marriage would be no more, or less, meaningful than any other love affair—and then he'd discovered she'd had no other love affair.

He was to be the first, and that fact added a dimension of solemnity, that he hadn't intended, to their marriage as well as a sense of responsibility that he wasn't sure he wanted.

But, after considering the situation, he'd seen that this was just one more reason why she was so right for him—and he for her. He would like for this experience to be perfect for her and he felt confident that he could make it so.

He rubbed his palms together in anticipation. This was going to work out after all. And without any careless emotional entanglements. Just the way they'd agreed.

The moment she walked through the door, he knew that at the end of this evening he would not recall what they ate, what they talked about, what music was on the stereo.

Her formfitting gown was the green-gray color of the sea beneath the rain clouds. It was cut low across her breasts and clung precariously to her shoulders.

The fabric shimmered as she moved, accentuating her small waist and feminine hips. The hem stopped at her knees. The shape of her calves, clad in pink silk stockings, was redesigned by the high heels she wore.

Like a man in a trance he approached her. "Selena," he murmured. "Words escape me."

She laughed—the soft, husky sound enchanted him—and shook her head. He could smell the familiar scent of her shampoo. Her hair spilled across her shoulders and was held away from her face on one side by the tiny butterfly clasp.

"Thank you, Nicholas."

Saber realized that was the perfect response. She didn't demur, she didn't deny, she didn't dismiss the compliment. Though his wife lacked vanity, she did have a healthy self-confidence, and tonight she knew she was beautiful.

She'd called him Nicholas. How odd, he thought.

She looked around at the candlelit scene. "The table looks lovely."

He shook himself mentally and dragged his eyes away from her. "Shall we?" He held her chair and she sat down.

Before he took his own seat he touched a bell, and the steward appeared immediately with the first course.

The evening had been wonderful. From the moment Selena had entered the salon and witnessed Saber's dumbfounded response to her appearance, she'd been overjoyed that she'd managed to engage his attention so completely. She had wondered if she would ever be able to accomplish such a thing.

And now they walked along the corridor toward their private quarters. Selena realized that her footsteps had begun to drag, so she deliberately quickened her pace. She was ready to cast aside the vague and silly timetable they'd set for themselves. Since Nicholas's admission of desire and clear demonstration of frustration this afternoon, she was eager.

Saber opened the door and stepped back for her to precede him. She took two steps inside and stopped. He came up behind her, standing close, but not touching her.

Selena took in a deep breath and held it.

He grinned at her back. "You look like you're being led to the guillotine."

He teased rather than reproached, but she was quick to deny his words. "No, I'm just wondering about the etiquette for this."

"Why don't you just relax and let me show you," he murmured softly from behind her.

Her bare shoulders had driven him crazy all night. They gleamed with alabaster perfection and he wondered if they could possibly be as smooth as they looked.

They were. He caressed her from her delicate collarbone to her upper arms. He bent his head to touch his lips to that delightful place where shoulder and throat and jaw met, and felt her shiver. He sensed correctly that she would feel more comfortable in familiar surroundings.

"Come," he said gently, leading her into her own bedroom rather than taking her to his. "We're going to take this very slowly."

* * *

In the pale light of dawn, Saber looked down at his wife. Her tousled hair was spread across his shoulder, her cheek rested against his chest. Under his arm he could feel her rhythmic breathing. To look at her she seemed relaxed. But there was something slightly off kilter, a remaining thread of anxiety that revealed itself in the angle of her shoulder, the position of her leg. Even in her sleep, she seemed to cling to a certain independence, as though she couldn't completely let go.

He sighed. Once more he found himself in the position of watching Selena without her being aware of it. The resulting disquiet was far greater than the last time. Before, when he'd watched her sunbathe on the day after their wedding, he'd been assaulted by physical desire. Today he was struck with a more dangerous and emotional reaction that was difficult to deny. That day his body had been moved; now, his heart was moved, and he could not afford that.

He eased himself away from the sleeping woman and got out of bed. He reached for his robe and left the room. *Pull yourself together,* he cautioned. Coffee, he needed coffee, hot and strong and black. He went in search of some.

For years he had buried himself in his work. He couldn't afford the distraction of love; he would not live with the vulnerability that intimacy demanded.

These days were like a block out of time; they would soon pass and he had to be ready to reassume his duties.

Later. Later, when he was back at work, when his hours were filled, he'd be able to handle the emotions Selena had begun to provoke in him. Later, when he knew her better, he wouldn't be so fascinated.

When Selena awoke, the bed beside her was empty.

Her emotions were in a turmoil. Their lovemaking had been exquisite. Everything that should have happened did. But the experience also had been somehow oddly unfulfilling and she would have felt better about herself if he were here beside her.

She dragged herself into the shower. When she came out of the bathroom ten minutes later, toweling her hair dry, she felt marginally better.

Saber was waiting for her. "I brought us some coffee."

"Thank you." She wrapped her wet hair turban-style and took the cup he offered. He relaxed in a chair, his long legs stretched out in front of him, crossed at the ankle; his expression was closed and tight. But he was studying her very closely.

"You're not very happy this morning, are you?" he asked quietly.

"No, not very happy," she answered after a pause.

He sipped his coffee. "You were right when you wondered if we might be making a mistake. We should have waited," he said finally.

"Probably." Selena flashed him a glance, remembering the moment on the beach yesterday when she'd uttered those words. She wandered to the window and stood staring out at the overcast day. The color of the clouds matched her mood. Gray.

She noticed that he hadn't apologized for making love to her. Thank God for that, at least.

She eliminated all emotion from her features before she turned to look at him. His own expression was laced now with self-reproach as he met her steady gaze.

"Well, we were swept up in the moment, but it was a mistake we don't have to make again. There isn't a lot we can do about it now, is there?" she asked.

She thought she saw a smile—no, surely not. When he spoke she knew she'd been wrong. "No, there isn't a lot we can do about it," he agreed gruffly.

The cruise continued as before, except Saber was even more detached, more deeply engrossed in affairs of state. She saw him only at mealtimes. She wondered if he had given the captain an explanation for the tension and withdrawal, because surely the crew had noticed that the honeymoon couple were less than devoted.

But then she dismissed the idea. First, Saber wasn't the kind of man to explain himself. And second, the crew members were much too well disciplined to talk about their president's personal life. They probably felt sympathy for the poor man who had to work even on his honeymoon. And finally—there wasn't the media pressure here to know every detail of a dignitary's life. Thank goodness.

At least on the yacht they were isolated, protected from the real world and its very real pressures. Soon they would have to forfeit that luxury for the jobs each of them had to do, jobs that would complicate their already complicated lives and push them even further apart.

Neither of them was ready yet to reenter that real world. But both of them knew it couldn't be avoided.

Chapter Seven

When the yacht docked at midnight, ten days from the day Saber and Selena had set sail, there were a few journalists hanging around the gate to the harbor. But they were stringers, sent there to wait, since the time of arrival hadn't been announced. Their presence was not a nuisance; a few pictures of the smiling couple and they were satisfied.

One of the photographers remarked on Selena's newly acquired tan, and a reporter questioned Saber about the fine-arts exchange program with Italy. Incidental matters, Selena was relieved to note, as they got into the waiting car.

The drive to the palace was completed in silence. Selena was apprehensive about settling into a new routine, and she wondered what would be expected of her.

Saber showed her to her quarters and when their luggage had been delivered, he dismissed both the driver and the housekeeper who had been there to greet them. "I'll show my wife around," he told her. "Thank you."

Selena had barely had time to respond to the introduction, but she didn't miss the sharp, unsmiling look the woman gave her. She wondered about that.

At one time, Saber explained, these had been the queen's rooms and the floor plan was identical to his apartment. But there hadn't been a queen in the palace for over thirty years. This space was usually reserved for visiting guests.

Except for the sound of his voice and their footsteps, Selena hadn't, until this moment, thought about the fact that she was to be left, more or less, on her own. True, Saber had told her that she would have her own apartment for the first few weeks. But for some reason the idea of such seclusion hadn't registered. At least on the yacht there had been people close by; here she felt totally isolated. "Is there going to be speculation about our living apart?" she asked.

He was silent for a minute. "No. The housekeeper sees to this area of the palace. She wouldn't allow anyone to work here who was a gossip."

Selena listened and observed as Saber showed her through the apartment. Decorated in shades of burgundy and garnet, and tones of gold, the rooms were sumptuous and ornate. The fabrics were heavy—damasks, velvets and thick-weaved silk tapestries. The woods—mahogany, teak and ebony—were dark. She found the rooms very formal and cold—and depressing.

"The O'Haras stayed here during the wedding," Saber told her as he prepared to leave.

"I'll bet Bree and Ryan loved this," she muttered.

To her surprise, he chuckled and let his gaze roam over the room. "Bree said the place reminded her of a dungeon. You're welcome to make changes. I'm nearby, right down the hall, if you need me." He hesitated. "Actually there used to be a door between our apartments but it was closed off when the remodeling was done and these became guests' quarters. I hope you'll be comfortable here, Selena."

"I'm sure I will be."

They were standing beside a dining table with seating for six. He looked around for a minute, as though he were at a loss. "I have a breakfast meeting scheduled for tomorrow morning. One of the appointment secretaries will come by to talk to you and I'll try to see you at lunch." He snapped his fingers. "No, I forgot. I'll be tied up then, too."

She was suddenly very tired. She wished for a woman friend, for her mother, or even for Bree O'Hara, someone who might understand her feelings of abandonment.

At last she spoke, not caring whether or not he sensed her discouragement. "Don't worry about it, Saber. I'll look for you when I see you. Good night." She turned her back on him.

Saber studied her back for a minute. Her shoulders were unnaturally straight, her body too still. Why did he have this feeling of guilt, this feeling that he was deserting her? This was what she wanted, what they both needed—space and time. Wasn't it?

"Good night, Selena," he said finally. "I'll see you sometime tomorrow."

The rooms that Selena occupied weren't far from Saber's apartment but they might as well have been at the other end of the country, thought Selena, as she stood staring out over the courtyard.

For the past two weeks she had only the most cursory contact with her husband. Sometimes he seemed to regret not being able to spend more time with her; other times he seemed grateful to escape. What contact they did have was usually in the company of others, or was rushed and hurried because Saber was on his way somewhere else. He spent several nights out of town.

He was working to catch up on all the meetings he'd postponed during their wedding and honeymoon. With the exception of that one fatal day, he'd worked steadily during the cruise. However, she had no illusions, not since the diplomatic dinner in Washington—the night she'd decided to accept his proposal—that his duties ever slackened.

She had gotten her first look at her own schedule on the morning after their return from the cruise, when a secretary appointed by the council of ministers entered her sitting room.

It had been early, barely seven o'clock. She was glad she'd dressed before sitting down to breakfast because the man just barged right in without knocking.

"Madam Saber?"

His voice had startled her into spilling her coffee. "Yes, and who do you think you are?" she snapped, using her napkin to blot the brew off the table.

He had been unperturbed. "I am Charles Tyron, secretary to the council of ministers. I have here—"

"Mr. Tyron, it is quite early," Selena had interrupted sharply, ignoring the papers he was waving in her face. "I don't know what it is you want but I have not yet had my coffee, and I do not appreciate your barging into my quarters without knocking."

"I do apologize," he had said stiffly, not looking the least bit sorry. "I assumed you would be ready to receive. Karastonian women—"

"I am an American." She realized immediately that she had said the wrong thing. He straightened his shoulders and peered down his nose at her.

She, in turn, looked him over carefully. He was tall, as thin as a reed and pitifully humorless. He reminded her of Ichabod Crane. Wire-rimmed glasses sat on the end of his nose. He peered over the rims instead of through the glass and she wondered why he bothered to wear them in the first place.

That morning, they had met for fifteen minutes. During that time, Charles Tyron had also taken her downstairs to show her the space that had been set aside for her temporary use until a proper office could be prepared. It was a tiny little cubical—two desks, two chairs, one filing cabinet. She hoped they didn't have to spend much time together there.

The schedule, which he presented to her, was already set in concrete, it seemed. She asked once, when he was telling her about a ribbon cutting at the new wing of the hospital to be followed by a luncheon with the nursing staff, if she would have time to visit some of the patients. He was horrified that she would even *think* about meddling with his precious schedule.

She found, as the days passed, that the events he scheduled for her were entirely ceremonial, nothing of substance, nothing she could get her teeth into.

On another occasion, she inquired about possibly speaking to the government classes at the university. That was when she learned that the ratio of women to men in the College of History and Political Science was somewhere around one to fifty. Tyron told her this grudgingly in order to explain why she might lack credibility in speaking to a class comprised of men.

Selena kept her temper with the greatest resolve.

It took only a few days, also, for Selena to discover that Charles Tyron didn't like to have to explain himself. He always listened to her questions with minimal tolerance and a hint of boredom. If she offered an idea, he promised to bring it to the attention of his superiors. If she followed up, he evaded the topic.

Perhaps he didn't like his job any more than she liked him.

She decided that if Saber wanted her to contribute, he was going to have to let her have some leeway in planning her own schedule. She had always handled her own correspondence, but she could see from the number of letters that had been handed to her that she needed her own secretary, someone she could actually talk to in a conversational exchange, not a barrage of words from one side that barely pierced the surface of the mind of the other.

She had mentioned the idea of a personal secretary to Saber during lunch yesterday. He'd agreed readily to her idea of offering the job to her cousin, Alia.

As soon as they finished lunch she had telephoned Alia's home, only to be told that Alia was in the

United States, visiting Selena's parents for a few days. That news caused a wave of homesickness to wash over her. She left a message.

She was also thrust quickly into another dilemma, this one on an entirely different level. The housekeeper who took care of their apartments had been the maid to Saber's first wife.

Selena was treated constantly to long, evaluating looks from the woman, to heavy sighs and oblique remarks about Lisha's youth and beauty and sweetness.

After one of those experiences, Selena found that she was unusually grouchy for the rest of the day. She realized that the emotion which prompted her crankiness was jealousy. She had never been jealous before and the feeling unsettled her.

After two weeks of the stifled atmosphere, she steeled herself to confront Saber at the first opportunity. She discovered that opportunity was as elusive as a hummingbird. But she had to do something.

Saber seemed to be treating her as the men of Karastonia had treated their women for centuries—protectively, like chattel, like possessions—and she would not stand for it.

Saber wanted her to be a new role model, he'd said, for the new Karastonian woman. How could she be one, when he seemed content to leave her in the archaic past?

At last a day arrived when she thought she might have a chance to be alone with him. She rechecked the schedule and dressed carefully for a dinner with the Italian ambassador. But rather than present herself at the reception room at the proper time, she left her apartments early and went the short distance down the hall to Saber's rooms. She knocked on his door.

He opened it himself. His hair was damp from the shower and she could smell the scent of something fresh and outdoorsy. Onyx studs were in place in his shirt but the ends of his black tie dangled loosely and one of his cuffs was open.

"Selena." He was clearly surprised. He fumbled with his cuff, trying to insert the cuff link. "Come in. Is something wrong?"

"Yes, Nicholas. Something is definitely wrong. You're avoiding me."

"Don't be silly, Selena. You haven't mentioned a problem. Damn." The last was directed to his cuff, which he was struggling to fasten.

Without thinking, she took the cuff link from him and tended to the task. "No, because I didn't want to bother you." Drat, why should she apologize? "That is, you didn't seem to have the time to listen."

Saber's eyes narrowed as he stared down at the shining head. She had pulled her hair back into an intimidating bun. He liked it loose. She wore a subdued black dinner dress; he preferred her in colors.

He realized suddenly that he was looking for things to criticize, for his own self-protection. The brush of her fingers against the skin of his wrist was soft and warm. Her scent was floral and spicy, very appealing. He could feel the awakening of his desire.

He shook himself mentally. "I'm sorry if you had that impression. I'll always have time to help you with a problem." She had finished fixing his cuff. He put a hand to her chin to make her look at him. He heard the huskiness in his voice when he continued, "But you have to mention it first. I am not a mind reader, Selena.''

Their gazes locked but whatever might have been said was interrupted by a knock at the door.

With a sigh, Saber left her and went to answer. He talked for a moment and then closed the door again. ''The ambassador is not feeling well tonight and asks to be excused.''

''Oh, I'm sorry.'' The man had served with her father years ago in Washington, when they were both young embassy clerks. ''I'll call on him tomorrow, if you'd like.''

''That would be kind of you.'' He hesitated. ''I've asked the staff to serve dinner up here. Do you mind?''

''No,'' she said quietly. But her surprise was tempered with glee. Maybe now she could straighten out a few matters.

An hour later, Selena threw her napkin down on the table in disgust. ''Don't be sarcastic with me, Saber. I don't need this. I may have to put up with that Ichabod Crane of a secretary, but I don't—'' At his warning glance, she broke off. The butler removed her plate and set a compote of sherbet before her.

When he had gone she continued, ''I don't feel that I'm contributing to the women of Karastonia. All I've done is cut ribbons. Anyone can cut ribbons.''

Was that a hint of a smile at the corner of his mouth? ''And what is the solution?''

''Well, you're the president and I don't want to go on with any plans without consulting you, but you're never around when there's a decision to be made.''

He sighed tiredly. "Selena, I can't help that."

"I know. I'm not asking that you be at my beck and call. But how can I do the things that you seemed to want me to do..." She let her voice trail off. When she spoke again it was stronger. "You do still have a use for me, don't you? You didn't get me here under false pretenses?"

"Don't be silly. Of course I didn't. I have just been unusually busy since our return...."

"The year is going to end eventually, Nicholas."

His gaze was instantly drawn to her but she didn't notice. An idea had suddenly occurred to her. "I may have a solution," she said thoughtfully. "What I propose is this—" She linked her fingers together and propped her chin on them. "It's an idea I borrowed from my parents. You know, Nicholas, it wasn't easy on them when they were first married. Daddy was gone a lot and so was Mother. You may not know that they separated once."

He raised a brow. "No, I didn't know that."

"Yes, despite the fact that *they* were in love, their marriage was in trouble." She let her lids fall slightly to hide her response to the flare in his eyes. "The point is, marriage isn't easy under the most ideal conditions."

He did smile then and she realized how ridiculous that sounded. She had never been married; he had. He spoke before she could continue.

"I agree that it is very difficult for two people, two independent people," he amended, "to join their lives. I'd be interested to know how Turnus and Jayne handled the conflict."

"They allowed at least one hour a day for each other. They set the time for eight o'clock in the evening, or thereabouts. Sometimes it was the hour before and sometimes the hour after. If they were in the same city, of course they were together alone and face-to-face."

Selena paused and smiled, then continued, "Many times, though, their date had to be over the telephone. But they set aside that hour for themselves, and they vowed that nothing would interfere with it. If Father had a diplomatic function to attend or if Mother had a booking, they worked it out. If we were all at home, I knew that their hour together was inviolate. I have an idea they didn't always talk."

Saber eyed her speculatively. "How interesting," he said.

"Saber, I know that we're not even sure that our marriage will last. But, even if it doesn't, I don't want my time here to be useless. I love this country. Maybe if we can talk together regularly..."

"All right."

She was just getting wound up to argue in favor of her suggestion. His statement took the wind out of her sails. "What?"

"I said all right. We'll make a date for every night at eight o'clock."

"And no matter what—"

"No matter what. We'll meet together if at all possible. If not, we'll speak on the telephone, and we'll talk about whatever we want or need to discuss. It's a good idea, Selena."

He was really pleased, she thought with some surprise. She smiled with satisfaction. "Thank you, Nicholas."

"Is there anything else bothering you?"

She was hesitant at first but, at his urging, she finally told him about the situation at the university. "One thing...from something you said when you asked me to marry you. I think we should have a major push for registering women to vote. That would generate some interest in the subject. I could arrange for you to do some public-service announcements that would appeal especially to women."

He seemed to pick up on her enthusiasm. "That is a very good idea. You must appear in it with me."

Time passed quickly and, for the time they spent together, they returned to the easy camaraderie they'd shared the first night of their marriage.

There was one other item she wanted to talk about, but she hesitated. The hour was late; she would have to go soon. Finally, she decided to take the chance. "Nicholas," she ventured, "how important is Mr. Tyron to you?"

The question surprised him. "He's been with me for a number of years. Why?"

"If Alia decides to go to work for me, I don't think I'll need anyone else. You probably depend on him for more important duties."

Saber's eyes narrowed. "The truth, Selena. What's happened?"

She sighed heavily. "The truth is I'm having trouble working with a man who doesn't give me credit for having a feasible idea of my own. I've mentioned the voter registration campaign and a number of other issues to him, areas where I might be of help. He always comes up with a reason why they won't do. And then he sends me off to another ribbon cutting.''

Saber's eyes narrowed as she spoke; she saw a spark of anger there and hoped it wasn't directed at her. ''I'm sorry, Selena. Charles hasn't brought any of your ideas to me for consideration.''

She wasn't really surprised to hear that. ''Then I'll make a list for you.''

He nodded. ''Good.''

She glanced at her watch, though she knew exactly how late it was. ''Well, I guess I'll be going.''

His mouth lifted at one corner. ''I'll walk with you.''

Selena's first instinct was to decline his company, but she decided that would sound foolish. She tried for lightness in her voice. ''Thank you. I wouldn't want to be mugged on the way home.'' She preceded him out the door. The hall, as usual, was chilly and damp.

''Saber, have you ever thought of moving out of here? Of living in a real house?'' she said as they walked slowly along. She didn't know why she asked the question—she supposed as a conversational gambit—but she was surprised by his answer.

''I've never thought about it,'' he said evenly. ''I've lived in one part of the palace or another since the king gave me my first appointment when I was twenty-eight. It was convenient for him to have his people nearby. Now it's close to the governmental offices and convenient to the legislature, so I guess I'm confined here for now.'' When they reached her door, he turned to look down at her. A strand of hair had escaped her chignon. He tucked it behind her ear.

She caught her breath when his warm fingers lingered on her neck. "You couldn't drive back and forth to work from another place?" she asked, hoping the effect of his touch was reflected in her voice.

"It's something to consider," he replied thoughtfully. "Why do you ask, Selena? Are you unhappy living here?"

She answered before she thought. "No more than any other place, I guess."

His face became closed to her, suddenly and completely.

"I'm sorry, Saber. I didn't mean that like it sounded," she said quickly. "I just—"

"Of course not," he said, cutting her off.

Before she could speak again he gave her a formal half bow. "I'll see you tomorrow night at eight, then. You'll have a list of other suggestions?"

"Yes, yes, of course," she said distractedly. "Saber, please . . ."

But he'd turned and walked away, leaving her standing there alone, staring at his back. Damn.

The courtyard was stark and deserted. Moonlight painted the paths silver, the grassy verge black, the marble stones white. Saber, still dressed in his formal clothes, harmonized with his setting. He strode determinedly along the perimeter next to the castle wall, like a man with a place to go. In reality he was trying to work off some of his frustration.

Selena's innocent question about leaving the palace had taken him by surprise. If he'd ever thought about a home of his own, it was an idea for the distant future. He would not want anything like the cold, formal house he'd grown up in or the palace where he'd spent most of his adult life, but a real home, comfortable, bright with light, on a bluff, overlooking the sea. With a garden.

Maybe someday, when his responsibilities were ended, he'd have such a place.

He thought about Selena's proposal that they spend a certain time together every day. It wouldn't be easy to arrange, not at first, not until he made it clear to his staff that he meant what he said when he told them he was not to be disturbed. They would eventually get the message, however.

Every night at eight. A smile spread over his features. This might work out well. He'd been reluctant to admit to himself that he was dissatisfied with their infrequent meetings. No matter that they were safer, he'd missed having her to talk to. Her intelligence was often a challenge, but she certainly never bored him.

He veered off the main path and onto a narrower one that led to a small cemetery, and without realizing it he came to a stop before his first wife's grave. He stood there for a long minute.

Lisha had been a sweet, lovely child and he had grieved over her death. He wondered what would have happened if she had lived. They would have grown apart; he was sure of it. She had been a clinger and he would have eventually disliked that. She had no concerns other than him, his home, their hope for a family. She had never taken an interest in his work, had seemed bored on the rare times when he'd mentioned it.

He would always have loved her, but one thing he knew—Lisha paled beside the image that rose to his mind now when he thought of Selena.

Lisha would not have understood his deep concern for his work, his occasional preoccupation, as Selena did—most of the time. Selena. He was married to a woman who was as different from Lisha as the sun is from the stars. Could he make her happy enough to stay here permanently? Or at least content enough?

Saber ran a tired hand around the back of his neck and plunged his hands in the pockets of his trousers. He let his back curve, his shoulders slump, his head drop forward in a posture of exhaustion and lassitude.

Selena looked out the windows of her apartment. Below, Saber was the picture of despair as he stood staring at the grave of his wife. Selena squeezed her hands together tightly until her fingers grew numb and she blinked in an attempt to clear her eyes of the tears that had sprung up without warning.

With a heart that felt like a lump of clay and a burning in the back of her throat, she turned away, unable to bear the sight of his grief any longer. She had been concerned about this and now she knew it was true—he would never get over Lisha.

And how did she feel about that, Selena asked herself. She'd come here with her eyes wide open. She knew their relationship was to be based on companionship, need, friendship. She'd never been deceived into thinking that he would love her.

But now she'd begun to suspect that she needed more, that marriage was a bad bargain without love or, at the very least, something that closely resembled that emotion.

Had she, deep down, wanted his love, subconsciously yearned for it? Had she foolishly pictured herself as the unawakened princess, to be roused with a kiss from the handsome prince? Admittedly, she'd had a crush on this man when she was very young. But a teenage crush rarely blossomed into a mature relationship.

She crossed the room with restless strides, stripping off her dress as she headed for the shower. She would make a place for herself in Karastonia or she would leave. It was that simple.

Saber had agreed to the daily contact, a good first step. Maybe some of the feelings she needed would result from that. She vowed to herself to make the most of those meetings. Then she would see what happened.

The interview with Alia went well. Selena had known her all her life but only as a much younger cousin with whom she shared family events.

Alia was as intelligent and ambitious as Selena had thought she might be. When Selena explained what she hoped to accomplish, the young woman responded with enthusiastic support and some ideas of her own. It was agreed that she would come to work at nine o'clock the following morning.

That evening, Selena was able to report to Saber that she was happy with her choice.

Saber had some news of his own, which he imparted with a slight grin. Charles Tyron had been reassigned and her liaison with the council of ministers, from now on, would be David Leandos, a man of her generation, whom she knew and liked.

She wondered if the man she thought of as Ichabod had requested the change or if Saber had ordered it. Nonetheless, she had a sneaky feeling that Charles Tyron was as happy as she was.

Chapter Eight

The dinner with the Italian ambassador, postponed for a week when he had come down with a virus, was rescheduled for tonight. Selena was looking forward to spending a quiet evening with her father's friend and his wife—and her own husband.

She wore a stylish gown of black lace with a modified heart-shaped neckline and long, tightly fitted sleeves, and she'd swept her hair into a chignon and misted herself with her favorite fragrance. She met her own gaze in the mirror. Would Saber like the way she looked tonight?

While she was dressing, she had slowly become aware of a disturbing feeling inside her, a strange, odd feeling, and one which put her on an emotional edge. She put her hand over her stomach to quiet the flutter there.

Occasionally their nightly meetings were in his apartments, occasionally in hers, which were more formally decorated. Tonight they were dining here; the ambassador and his wife would arrive later, but, for now, Saber was waiting in her living room.

One night earlier in the week, he'd had to be out of town and they'd talked on the telephone. True to his word, he'd called at exactly eight o'clock. But the instrument was oddly inhibiting and a poor substitute for a face-to-face meeting. They talked more freely and easily, and for a longer period of time when they were together.

The last few evenings spent with him had been— *productive,* her mind told her as she clasped her grandmother's pearl choker around her throat. *Enchanting,* said her heart. He was thoughtful, complimentary and—*reachable.*

She sensed that Saber was benefiting from their meetings, too. His schedule was as horrendous as ever; its effects were often visible in the lines of strain in his face, the shadows around his eyes. Most evenings he left her to return to his office—but he left more relaxed and refreshed than when he'd arrived.

As she was doing tonight, she'd dressed carefully each evening and, judging from Saber's reaction, he'd approved of her efforts. Of course, she had never gotten the stunned reaction of that unforgettable night on the yacht, but his appreciation was unmistakable.

She had also tried to prepare herself with something of importance to discuss with him. She still dreaded conversational lags. When she had no subject to focus on, she suspected that she might be revealing more about her personal feelings than she intended. Fortunately such lags were rare.

A few seconds later, she paused at the door to the sitting room and observed that Saber was more relaxed than she'd seen him. He had put some music on the stereo—cleverly hidden in an antique armoire— mixed himself a drink and now sat with his feet propped comfortably on an ottoman. She was heartened by his apparent relaxed mood as he waited for her.

This was what she'd hoped for, that he would begin to anticipate their meetings as something to look forward to. She watched him from the door. Then her eyes were drawn to the window. Her heart felt heavy as she recalled the scene beside his wife's grave.

He was about to drink from his glass when she moved into his line of vision. Her appearance halted his hand in midair. The relaxation that had stamped his features eased suddenly to an expression she couldn't read.

"Selena," he said softly, rising and coming toward her. He lifted a hand as though to touch her, and then let it drop back to his side.

He continued to stare at her until finally she tilted her head, looking at him quizzically. "May I get you a drink?" he asked.

She barely wavered. "Yes, please. I'll have a dry sherry."

He smiled and he did touch her then, just a fleeting brush of his fingers against her forearm, but she felt a tingle all the way to her toes. "You father would be pleased with your choice."

"You're right. Maybe I'm finished with rebelling."
She smiled. "Don't ever tell him this, but I happen to
like sherry." Her voice trailed off when she noticed
that he was preoccupied. "Saber, is something
wrong?"

He recovered quickly. "Nothing more than the
usual. Difficult day." He turned away to get her drink.
"How are things working out with your cousin?" he
asked as he handed her the glass.

"Alia has quite a creative mind. I'm pleased with
her."

"And the plans for your classes at the university?
Are the officials still giving you difficulty?"

He was clearly filling time. Selena's curiosity was
aroused. Still she hesitated, remembering the scene
they'd had the last time this subject was discussed.
Saber had been angered by the obstacles placed in her
way when she went to the university with her proposal. She wanted to teach an adult-education course
on government, specifically aimed toward women.

The structure of her curriculum had to be approved, however, by the university officials and, while
they acknowledged her doctorate in world history,
they had questioned her expertise on the structure of
the new Karastonian government.

Saber had wanted to call up the president of the
university, order the man to give her a position. After
all, he'd made her a promise. "You might as well be
back in that college in Virginia," he snapped as he'd
paced the floor of her office.

Selena had understood the school's wariness, however, and she'd tried to make him understand, too.

With some effort and a bit of amusement, she had managed to calm him down. "The king could have delivered such an order, Saber, but not you. This is what happens in a democracy," she had reminded him, provoking a wry grin. She'd gone on to explain, "Besides, they didn't turn me down. I'm going to take a competency test after the Independence Day observances are over. I have too much to do between now and then to spend all my time studying."

Saber had grumbled, but, since then, had helped her enormously by making sure she had easy access to all the information she needed. For the most part, the governmental structure of Karastonia was similar to that of the United States, but there were disparities. She would have to be letter-perfect if she wanted to satisfy the officials.

Now she answered his question carefully. "The university officials have been cautious, as they should be. I'll be ready for the test, Saber. I'm not worried." She lifted her eyes to meet his gaze. Her mouth tilted wryly. "But I am apprehensive about the class offering in the fall. It would be embarrassing if no one wants to take my course."

He chuckled. "You underestimate yourself, Selena."

"I hope you're right." She shrugged. "I'd hate to be faced with an empty classroom."

He raised one brow; a corner of his mouth lifted. "You could insist that Alia take your course. That's one. I may not be king, but if I put my mind to it I could probably come up with several more names."

"That's an idea," said Selena. Encouraged by his humor, she laughed suddenly. "In fact, now that you mention it, I could fill the class with my relatives," she teased. "Why didn't I think of that?"

Saber turned his glass slightly for a minute, held it to the light. The amusement, what there was of it, had disappeared from his expression and he cleared his throat. "Speaking of our Independence Day observances, I have something to ask of you. A favor," he said without meeting her eyes.

"Certainly, Saber."

"We are going to be rather crowded around here during the festivities. Our first guests will begin arriving soon. I wonder if you would mind moving in with me so we can use these apartments for some of the visitors."

His expression, when he finally looked at her, was inscrutable. She had no idea how he really felt— whether he wanted her there or was expecting her to offer another solution. Of course, there were other bedrooms in his apartment. She could have all the privacy she needed or wanted.

She tried to keep a lighter, casual tone to her voice. "No, I wouldn't mind." Tomorrow would be a good day, she decided, running over her schedule in her mind. "I'll start packing in the morning." She watched him over the rim of her glass.

An expression she couldn't interpret flared briefly in his gaze. "Fine." He smiled quietly.

The ambassador was charming, his wife was witty and the dinner went well. At the end of the evening, Saber's mood was mellow as he stood by Selena's side. They had bid good-night to their guests and now Saber was preparing to leave. They were laughing easily over an anecdote the ambassador's wife had told at dinner.

Saber opened the door to the hall, paused, folded his arms across his chest and leaned a shoulder against the jamb. "I enjoyed this evening, Selena. I've enjoyed all the evenings we've spent together."

"I've enjoyed them, too." Silence fell between them as her smile diminished, but it was not an uncomfortable silence. The easy ambience of the evening remained for a few moments. But then it began to fade, to be replaced by a developing sense of anticipation.

They both became aware of it at the same time. As Saber straightened from his relaxed posture, Selena smoothed her skirt. She met his gaze, then looked away. "Well, I suppose I'd..."

The words stuck in her throat when he laughed aloud, an odd laugh, one with no humor. He reached out to slide his hand around her waist. "One of the first things I observed about you was that, when you are nervous, you begin your sentences with *well*." His voice was low, very low, and husky as he pulled her forward and into his arms. "Are you nervous about something, Selena?"

"Nervous?" she murmured. She could have objected to the embrace, but she didn't. She let herself be molded against his hard body.

His fingers splayed over her lower back. He didn't hold her tightly but the restraint seemed to cost him some effort. His head dipped; his warm lips brushed hers briefly. He tasted of rich, dark wine.

She knew suddenly that she wanted this, wanted it with surprising intensity. Her eyes drifted shut; she waited, expecting him to deepen the kiss. Instead he muttered, "It's been too long since I've kissed you."

His breath was warm against her lips. She opened her eyes. "Ah-h. Yes, it has," she answered softly. His gaze was dark and unfathomable. She realized that her arms were around his neck, her fingers in his hair.

Then he kissed her again. And again it was brief and light.

She really longed for a kiss that sparked the sensation she'd felt on the yacht, a take-charge, lusty, authoritative kind of kiss. She could feel the tension in him and she waited, her anticipation underscored by the heat radiating from his body, by his purely masculine scent.

At last she could bear it no longer. "You can do better than that," she said huskily. She tightened her arms around his neck and pulled his head down.

And then his mouth covered hers, hard and hungry, and totally satisfying. Their surroundings faded away; it seemed as though they were encapsulated in a world all their own.

When, at last, he raised his head to look at her, that dark gaze was slightly unfocused and his breathing was ragged and unsteady. He searched her expression as though for an omen, a sign of some kind.

She felt as though she might drown in those shadowy eyes. The silence between them was thick and heavy and she felt compelled to break it. "Nicholas." That was all she said—just his name, softly.

But the word had a strange effect; she could see him reestablish command of himself. The metamorphosis was swift. In seconds he was in complete control again. He smiled a suitable smile, said a conventional good-night and left rather abruptly.

She stood in the door watching him go, her eyes stinging for some reason. She wished she hadn't been so impatient, hadn't broken the silence.

The next morning Selena asked Alia and the housekeeper to help her pack and move her things into Saber's apartment. The housekeeper spent the morning in grudging assistance. There seemed to be approval in her attitude, though, something Selena hadn't seen before.

Alia, on the other hand, was helpful but preoccupied.

"Is something bothering you, Alia?" Selena finally asked when they were alone.

Alia looked at her, then away. "No, nothing," she said quickly.

Too quickly. "If you need to talk I hope you'll consider me a willing listener and a friend."

"Yes, I will," said the young woman quietly. "But, I'm fine. Really."

Well, that's all I can do, Selena thought, studying the girl. She couldn't force Alia to share what was obviously a personal problem.

"There is something I would like to ask you," Alia blurted out fifteen minutes later, taking Selena by surprise.

Selena paused, a sweater in her hand. "Yes?"

"I've learned much from you about American women..." Her voice trailed off. "How would you, uh, do you think—" Her voice rose on a note of panic and she turned away again. "What do you think about the practice of arranged marriages?" she finally asked.

Oh, dear, thought Selena. Her cousin was definitely of marriageable age. She was hit suddenly with the suspicion that Alia's parents were pressuring her to marry someone she didn't like. Perhaps for a dowry— she knew that they lived very simply. "Are you speaking generally or from special interest?" she asked gently.

Alia shrugged. "I suppose I mean generally." She seemed to be holding her breath as she waited for Selena to answer.

Which really meant that Selena's suspicions were correct. "I wouldn't accept it for myself, of course," said Selena. "The idea of someone else making a lifetime commitment in my name, maybe to someone I couldn't like—" she shook her head "—I couldn't do it."

Alia turned back and for the first time Selena saw the tears. "It isn't that I don't like him. I haven't met him yet."

Selena's jaw dropped. "Your parents are arranging a marriage with a total stranger?" she demanded, aghast at the idea.

All at once Alia's chin lifted. "He's from a fine family. I am very lucky. And I am going to meet him tonight. He is coming to our house for dinner."

Now the girl seemed to be defending the practice. The unexpected turnaround surprised Selena even more. She searched her mind for the right thing to say. But before she could speak at all, the housekeeper reentered the room.

Alia shot her a warning, pleading glance that she could easily understand. The subject would have to be dropped for now.

Selena was grateful for the interruption; she had no idea what her response would have been.

By six-thirty that evening, Selena had moved everything into Saber's apartment and was settled. More or less. Living in such close quarters was going to be a challenge.

Selena and Saber met in the sitting room at seven-thirty. She was wary; he seemed distracted; neither of them referred to the parting kiss last night.

Selena accepted a drink and sat down, but he prowled the room like a restless lion. Perhaps this was not the time...they made small talk for a moment. Finally Selena could contain herself no longer. "Saber, something came up today. I want to talk to you about it." She set her glass aside.

"Certainly," he answered, giving her his attention.

She described her conversation with Alia. There was a determined gleam in her eye as she concluded, "I didn't realize that such an antiquated custom was still widely practiced. It's a good thing we were interrupted because I probably would have given advice that my uncle wouldn't appreciate one bit." Restlessly she stood and walked away from him. Then she spun back and settled her hands on her hips. "Saber, how am I to encourage women to take responsibility for their lives, or to participate in the election process, if they are denied participation in a basic decision like whom to marry?"

Selena didn't notice that Saber's expression had clouded at her words. He went to the window to cover his inner predicament. "I doubt that Alia would be denied participation, Selena," he said carefully. "Her father wouldn't make her marry someone she didn't care for."

Again Selena began to pace. "She doesn't even *know* the man, Saber. How can she care for a total stranger?"

He watched her move with the grace that was so much a part of her. "And if she did know him?" he asked quietly. "Would that make a difference?"

"Not really. Most young people are a lot smarter than their parents give them credit for being. They should be able to choose their lifetime partners, don't you think?"

"I think that arranged marriages are often very, very happy," he said.

She glanced up to see that his expression had taken on that somber look she hated. It suddenly dawned on her—Saber's first marriage was arranged. "I'm sorry, Saber. Forgive me, I shouldn't have raised the subject."

The seriousness changed to puzzlement. "Nonsense. Why shouldn't you? No subject is taboo."

"Your first marriage. I know how much you loved Lisha—" Still did, if the demeanor she'd witnessed when he stood at Lisha's grave was any indication.

"Yes, I loved her," said Saber, fighting off his own feelings of guilt. "But, Selena, I was twenty, Lisha was eighteen. We certainly weren't mature enough to make that kind of decision for ourselves."

Selena cursed herself for bringing up the subject, now, just as they were beginning to make some progress in their own relationship. "Well, I'm sure there must be exceptions to every rule," she told him, hoping to ameliorate her earlier harshness. She laughed softly and shrugged. "But I would never forgive my father if he tried that on me again. Never."

A heavy silence descended on the room, a silence so profound that she could hear her own heartbeat. She realized that she'd made another mistake, but she couldn't, for the life of her, figure out what it was.

"Would you forgive the man?"

"Of course not, but the father is the major villain. A father should encourage his child to make the important decisions."

At last Saber gave a tired sigh. "Ah, Selena, I knew it would come to this someday." He looked at her, then raked his fingers through his hair and sighed again. "What if I told you, Selena, that Turnus and I did just that? Arranged this marriage?"

She swung to face him and stared, just stared, for a minute. Then she gave a nervous laugh. "I'd say you were teasing. Daddy wouldn't. Besides, you asked me yourself."

"Of course I did. But it's time you knew the truth, Selena. We promised each other honesty. I had worked out the details of our marriage with your father before I proposed to you. He knew I was thinking of marriage and he contacted me."

What was he saying? After last night... Selena had just begun to hope, to believe that he had some feelings for her... "No," she breathed. No, it couldn't be possible. Her father wouldn't have contacted Saber and offered her like a pig on a plate. Would he?

She searched Saber's features for a smile, a glimmer of amusement in his eyes, anything that would indicate he was not serious, that would refute his statement. But his expression was unreadable.

"You are serious, aren't you?" she whispered. God, she'd never known mere words could hurt so much. She put her fingers to her mouth; she felt tears gathering in her eyes and fought them back. "You lied to me."

"I am serious and, no, I haven't lied to you. I just didn't tell you all of the truth. My reasons for asking you to marry me were genuine. The only thing that you didn't know was that I had first arranged it with your father."

"And my conditions—you let me believe I was in charge of my destiny. While all the time it was a done deal. Tell me, Saber, was I one of a list of women you were considering?"

Saber winced. He couldn't let this go further. He caught her by the shoulders. "No, Selena. You're getting this all wrong. It was clear from the first that you were—*are*—the perfect wife for me. But if you had refused my proposal, neither your father nor I would have tried to push you. You made the decision yourself."

She could recall the scene clearly. He had made it all sound so appealing, the opportunity to help the women of Karastonia, the escape from an uncomfortable professional situation. Most appealing of all—she made herself face her true feelings, her real motives—was the chance to be married to a man she'd always been half in love with.

For when it came right down to it, she could have found another job, she could have helped the women, without resorting to marriage. She wanted to marry this man because she was in love with him. Maybe her feelings had all been subconscious, but they were finding the light of day now and she refused to deceive herself any longer.

So, what should she do about it? Could she compete with a dead woman for his affection? Would his feelings ever be as deep as hers? And could she live with him always knowing that she would never have his whole heart? That a part of his love would always be held in reserve for someone else?

"So," said Saber tightly, thrusting his hands into the pockets of his trousers and rocking slightly on his heels. "Now that you know the truth, do you want to be released from your commitment?"

"Released? You mean divorce?" She was horrified.

Instead of answering her question, he eyed her strangely and said, "I can understand your frustration. I shouldn't have kept this from you."

"Would you have told me?" she asked. Curiously, her initial anger had faded but she was still confused and stung. And hurt, so hurt. Why?

He looked at her, his expression ambiguous, his gaze intense with some emotion she couldn't identify. "I just did," he answered.

"I mean—" She waved her hand helplessly through the air. She didn't know *what* she meant and she refused to be provoked into making a decision while she was in such an emotional turmoil. She forced laughter into her voice to hide the hurt there. "I can't believe this." Maybe later when she was calmer she could think the situation through more clearly.

He took a step toward her. "Selena—"

She stood her ground and lifted her chin. "Well, at least you didn't lie about your feelings, Saber. I accepted from the first that this wasn't to be a romantic relationship."

Instantly, she wished she could have called back the words. They sounded too much like a challenge. When he spoke again she realized that he had taken them as one.

"If you got that impression, I must not have made myself clear," he said with a dangerous glint in his eyes. "Perhaps I should demonstrate again." He didn't give her time to protest; he pulled her into his arms. His hands spread suggestively over the curve of her hips. "I want you, Selena. I've wanted you since the day I flew to Virginia."

She tried to hold herself aloof but the moment he touched her she felt the warmth begin to spread along her spine. Deliberately, he moved her against him and she felt him, hard and demanding. Already her body was betraying her, relaxing in places where it shouldn't. She caught her breath. "That isn't romance," she murmured, mesmerized by his dark gaze.

He gave a deep chuckle, a satisfied, purely masculine sound that competed with the heavy drumbeat of her pulse. "It isn't?" he asked softly, nipping at her ear. "Then why do you feel so right against me? Why does the sight of you make my heart pound?" His breath was hot against her throat. "Don't you feel it, too?"

As though in a dream, she was floating and the only thing to cling to was Nicholas. Her fingers tightened on his broad shoulders; she turned her face, unconsciously searching for his mouth. But her self-protective instincts weren't completely lost. "It's only sexual," she whispered to herself.

He went completely still; she could feel the sudden tension that knotted his muscles into immobility. Then something seemed to snap in him like a tightly strung wire. For a heart-stopping moment, she thought he would move away.

Instead, keeping one arm around her, he swept the other beneath her knees and picked her up as though she were a cloud of down. "Then we might as well enjoy the sex," he growled. He crossed the lighted area, proceeded down the hallway and stepped into the obsidian blackness of her bedroom. The heavy door, propelled by his kick, settled into its frame with a thump.

He set her on her feet and his voice came out of the dark. Not softly romantic, no, definitely not. But thick with passion and desire. "If you don't want this, Selena, you'd better stop me now."

She hadn't realized how shallow her breath had become until she tried to garner enough for speech. She couldn't manage the words to tell him that she had no intention of stopping him, that she wanted him as much as he wanted her.

So, instead, she reached out for him through the darkness. Her fingers encountered the fabric of his shirt. Speech wasn't necessary, she discovered, as she found the buttons and began to free them.

Long before they reached the big bed, their clothes had—somehow—melted away. In the darkness, with the softness of satin-covered down beneath them, his touch was sure. He knew exactly where to kiss her, where to tease her lightly with a stroke of his clever fingers, where and when to caress more firmly.

In minutes her body was damp and singing, ready for him. He filled her smoothly, his breath escaping on a soft moan of satisfaction as she lifted toward him, accepting, eager. The tension built, gathering excitement from their rhythmic movements, perfectly in tune. Selena held her breath, feeling the anticipation grow, expand, increase to the level of infinite pleasure.

And suddenly spill over into ecstasy.

He called her name, a hoarse cry, and joined her in paradise.

Selena sighed softly when he rolled to his side, taking her with him, his strong arms wrapped tightly around her, his lips against her temple. Beneath her cheek she could hear his powerful heartbeat. She didn't think she had ever felt so secure, so protected, so... loved.

Slowly their bodies cooled; slowly their breathing returned to normal. She didn't know how much time had passed, but she was taken by surprise when Saber reached out and touched the switch beside the bed. She blinked at the sudden brightness.

Saber swung his legs to the floor, stood and reached for his clothes.

"Saber...?" Surely he wasn't leaving.

He smiled slightly but he didn't meet her questioning gaze. He checked his watch. "I have to make a run out to the airport. There's another problem on the border and the security chief is flying in from the north for a quick meeting."

Was it just her imagination or did he seem glad for the excuse?

Damon, the security chief that Saber had gone to meet, had to speak to him twice.

Saber was recalled to the present. Damn. He couldn't seem to concentrate, couldn't get his mind off Selena. Beautiful, sensuous, passionate Selena. His wife. God, he'd never felt like this.

He shook himself mentally and focused his attention on the man who stood at his side. They had been talking for over an hour. The man was ready to leave; the plane was waiting. And nothing had been resolved. "Try to keep Bafla calm for another few days, Damon," he said finally, speaking of the man who owned the large area near the border. "He sincerely believes that the monarchy should have been retained. But he isn't a difficult man at heart or a troublemaker."

"I know, Saber. He just wants personal appeasement from the president himself."

"And I don't have time for that right now. As soon as the formal celebration is over I'll come north and talk to him again."

Damon nodded. "I'll tell him that. Goodbye, Saber." He boarded the waiting plane.

Saber was chauffeured back to the palace, his mind still more on his wife and their relationship than on the

problems of the country. This was why he hadn't
wanted anything to do with emotional bonds. He
didn't *want* to fall in love.

He entered his quarters—*their* quarters now—and
halted to look at the door leading to his wife's room.
He'd learned quite a lesson earlier. His desire for her
had become impossible to control. The memory of
their lovemaking haunted him as he headed for his
own room.

Chapter Nine

The guests began to arrive; the palace was crowded. With the Independence Day celebration bearing down on them, Saber had given Selena—at her request—a list of extra tasks she could help with. During the days they saw each other only in passing. They did talk each night, but there was so much to be done that their meetings were abbreviated. They spoke mostly of business matters.

Selena told herself she was relieved; she had followed his lead—to steer clear of personal matters for now. She would rather keep things on a casual level until after the pressures of the holiday celebrations had eased. Then she was going to insist that they settle things between them. And she had a lot to say.

At first she had been hurt and confused. Why had he left so abruptly? She wasn't normally a weepy person, but tears often threatened to spill. She made sure they did so out of sight of anyone. When her confusion had cleared a bit, she realized that he'd been as overwhelmed as she by the force of their lovemaking. Her hurt turned to perplexity. She stopped crying and started thinking.

The formal schedule for the capital city was spread across her desk. She and Alia had been working since early morning.

The schedule had been approved months ago, but there were a number of regional committees that had decided to organize local celebrations, as well. They wanted guidelines to insure that their festivities would be in keeping with the rest of the country. What they really wanted was reassurance, thought Selena, and that was easy enough to provide. With each letter, she intended to enclose a copy of her own ideas for encouraging women to register to vote.

At eleven-thirty she yawned and told Alia that she thought she'd leave for an early lunch. "These letters are ready to be typed. I'll be back in time to sign them so we can get them in the afternoon's mail."

Saber was in their apartment, packing hurriedly. He called out to her to come and help.

"Thank you," he said when she took the shirt he'd been folding and made a neat package out of it. While they worked he explained that he had been called to the border on a mission that couldn't be postponed.

She knew that Saber had planned to visit there after the holiday. The same large landholder on the northern border who had given him trouble in the past had been stirring again, he explained. "Bafla is threatening voluntary annexation to a neighboring country. He's been a problem since the democratization process began. If I allow him to, he will lead others in the move. I realize it's the worst possible time, but I have to go. Do you think you can—"

She interrupted. "Don't worry about things here. I'll manage."

Saber stopped what he was doing and took her by the shoulders. "Thank you," he said again. He smiled, a tender smile. The last time she'd seen him smile that way was the night... She took a step into his arms. He bent his head but before his lips reached hers there was a discreet cough from the doorway.

The housekeeper apologized and grinned—the woman actually grinned. "Excuse me. Your driver is here. He says the car is ready, sir," she said.

Saber tightened his arms about Selena. "I'll be gone for one, possibly two nights. I'll call you." He kissed her then, but the kiss ended too quickly. Selena watched him go. When he was away the time passed slowly.

After a solitary lunch, she went into the bedroom to rest for a few minutes. She was so tired lately, she thought, with some surprise. She was rarely tired. "I hope I'm not coming down with something," she murmured to herself as she drifted off to sleep.

When the telephone rang three hours later she awoke disoriented and groggy. It was Alia, calling from her office downstairs to ask if Selena wanted her to bring the letters to her to be signed.

"No, no." She scraped her hair away from her face and looked at the clock in astonishment. She couldn't believe she'd slept so long. "I'll be down in a few minutes."

The deep sleep in the middle of the day scared her a bit. It was so unlike her. Again she wondered if there was flu going around.

Saber hadn't called; it was nearly nine. When the phone finally rang, Selena snatched up the receiver. "Hi," she said breathlessly.

There was a brief pause, and then amusement in his voice when he spoke. "Hi, yourself. You must have been sitting right beside the telephone."

She didn't want to give the impression she'd been living to hear the sound of his voice, but she had. It was difficult to sound blasé when her heart was spinning in her chest.

"I'm sorry to be late calling. Hold on a minute." He put his hand over the receiver. She could hear his muffled tones but not what he was saying. When he came back on the line he sounded impatient. "Selena?"

"I'm still here. How are things going?" she asked.

"Bafla, the man I came to see, has gone out of town." She could hear the anger in his voice.

"After you traveled all that way?" Selena said, her voice rising. She was angry, too, on his behalf. "That's rude."

He chuckled again. "You're damned right. The explanation is that he was called away to deal with an emergency, but clearly he's decided to avoid a face-to-face meeting. I should be home tomorrow but I'll have to come back here next week."

"So it was a wasted trip. I'm sorry."

"I am, too. Anyway, I'll see you tomorrow. Good night, Selena."

Selena's parents had called that morning to congratulate Saber. They were unable to get to Karastonia for the celebrations. Selena would have been more disappointed if she hadn't hoped to see them soon.

She had a few things to say to Turnus, not that it would do any good.

"Saber, as soon as the holiday is over, I would like to go home for a visit. I'll probably leave day after tomorrow. Do you mind?" she asked.

They were having breakfast together. The ceremonies commemorating the Independence Day festivities were to be held this afternoon.

He had been out late last night again, meeting with a trade representative from the United States. She didn't know what time he'd returned last night, but this morning she was foolishly glad to be able to have breakfast with him.

Slowly he set down his coffee cup and looked at her. There was an odd expression on his face. He stared fixedly, until she squirmed slightly.

"If the timing isn't convenient for you, Saber, I can wait a week or so."

"But you will go?"

"Yes, of course," she said, surprised. She couldn't imagine what his problem was. She smiled, deciding that this was an appropriate time to share her suspicion. "I need to—"

"And do you plan to return?" he questioned bluntly.

She hesitated. The harshness of the interruption saddened her, especially in light of what she'd been about to tell him. Her feelings were hurt, but she'd be damned if she let him see. "I thought I would," she said coolly. Distress was churning inside. "Why? Would you rather I didn't?"

He tossed his napkin down and stood. "Don't be ridiculous, Selena."

"Ridiculous? Thanks a lot, Saber." She would have said more but he turned on his way out the door to glare at her.

"I'll see you at the parade," he said, and left.

These little episodes were growing more and more frequent. She was still muttering to herself when she entered her office a few minutes later. The first thing she noticed was a huge bouquet of flowers on Alia's desk. The second was the dreamy look in the young woman's eyes.

Selena shook her head, smiling at the fickle heart. Antonio must be something indeed. She and Alia had been too busy in the office for the past few days to talk much about the man Alia's parents had selected for their daughter. But she'd heard enough to realize that Antonio was the kindest, most handsome, intelligent man in the land. Clearly theirs was one arranged marriage that might work out.

Absently, Saber answered the woman on his left, but seconds later he couldn't have repeated her question. Selena, at his right, totally occupied his mind.

She wanted to go home, she'd said. *Home.* He'd hoped that by now she could have begun to think of Karastonia as her home. Clearly she didn't.

When she'd introduced the subject this morning, the room had tilted on its axis, the atmosphere had become charged—from his point of view, at least. But his wife was blithely unaware that his whole world had changed in the blink of an eye. He loved her. And the thought of her leaving was like a stone in his chest.

God, what a fool he'd been! He'd assumed he could bring this strong, vital woman here and *not* fall in love with her—no matter how hard he fought it.

It had been extremely difficult for him to hide his reaction to her request. He didn't want her to go. It was as simple as that. Only his pride had kept him from begging her not to.

Once she said that she would return, he was appeased, but only slightly. She could very well get back to the States and decide to stay. And there wouldn't be a damned thing he could do about it.

He'd forced an indifferent smile as he'd agreed to her trip. But she would never know what the detachment had cost him. Her request—hell, it wasn't a request, it was an announcement—had festered inside of him all morning long like a sore place that refused to heal.

He realized unexpectedly that he was tired. He accepted the salutes, returned the smiles, tried to muster enthusiasm for the celebrations, but he found it difficult.

A place of his own, an uncomplicated, settled—but still productive—life-style. He'd never had such things. Never thought he needed them. Until Selena.

He was not going to run for president again. He'd made that decision a few days ago. He'd do what was expected of him for the time left in his term, and, if they wanted him, he would stay active in a consulting capacity. But that was it.

His parents would be horrified if they had lived to see this. But he knew now that he didn't want the cool, respectful kind of relationship they'd had. He wanted to be able to talk to his wife when he felt the urge, not just for one hour every night. He wanted a real marriage and he intended to have it.

If she came back, reminded a small voice in the back of his mind. The subconscious suggestion annoyed him.

As she looked out over the crowd, Selena smiled to herself. Except for the colors and design of the flag, she might have been attending a Fourth of July celebration in small-town America, complete with bands and banners, songs and sunshine, food and frolic.

Of course, in small-town America she would not be sitting beside her husband in the reviewing stand, watching the parade as first lady of the land. She would be happy to be just where she was if Saber's disposition weren't so mercurial. She had suddenly thought. Maybe he didn't *want* her to come back.

An aide approached her husband and whispered in his ear. She saw a dark expression cloud his features, and she wondered what had happened now. In a low voice he gave instructions to the man, who then nodded and disappeared into the crowd.

Daylight was fading when the last band marched past. Saber escorted her from the box toward the limousine for the short ride back to the palace. They moved unhurriedly through the crowd, speaking to various people.

To look at Saber, none of the people around would know that anything was wrong. But Selena realized that he'd had bad news.

The tension was palpable in the limousine, especially when she noticed his suitcase on the seat beside the driver. "You're leaving right now?"

He nodded. "As soon as I drop you off, I have to go back to the border. I'm sorry I'll have to skip our talk tonight, Selena."

"We have guests coming for dinner, Saber," she said, unable to believe that whatever it was couldn't wait until the morning. Or... maybe he wanted to go, maybe this was an excuse to get away from her. How much business could you accomplish at night, she wondered bitterly.

"Damn it, Selena, I thought you'd understand. You'll have to handle this on your own. I can't socialize when a corner of the country may be breaking off."

She was being unreasonable, she knew, but her disappointment was great. She'd wanted to tell him then, on that important day, on the first anniversary of the birth of the country's democracy, that she thought she was pregnant with their child.

After the chilly conversation at breakfast, she'd steeled herself to wait until evening. And now he was telling her that he had to leave. "How long will you be gone?" she asked stiffly.

"I don't know. I'll call you tomorrow night at the same time."

The limousine came to a smooth halt at the door to the palace. "If I'm still here," she said as the chauffeur opened the door and helped her out.

Like a shot, Saber was out of the car after her. He grabbed her arm and spun her to face him. "It isn't my choice to leave tonight, Selena," he said through gritted teeth.

The driver stood at attention holding the door. Selena felt sorry for the poor man, obviously trying very hard to be invisible.

"I thought you'd be more understanding," he accused, straining to keep his voice low.

"I do understand," she answered woodenly. Then she relented slightly. "I'll be here tomorrow night. Have a safe trip."

He dropped her arm and she started up the steps. She didn't watch the limousine pull away.

The next night at nine o'clock Selena sat beside the telephone, waiting for it, willing it, to ring. She could not believe that Saber was doing this to her.

She glanced at the clock again an hour later and wondered desperately if this marriage had a chance. Was he really that angry? She'd simply said she wanted to go to Virginia for a few day. How could he accuse her of not planning to come back?

And the progress she'd made here. Did he think that was unimportant to her?

They had a lot to talk about. Damn it, why didn't he call?

Nicholas raked his fingers through his hair, which was already standing on end. He hadn't slept in forty-four hours. His eyes were red-rimmed and swollen.

"What the hell is the matter with them?" he demanded, indicating the bank of telephones on the desk. "I *have* to get through. I have an extremely important call to make." He glanced at his watch, though he knew exactly what it read. He was four and a half hours late in calling Selena. She'd said she would be there tonight, but he'd be willing to wager that if he didn't call, she'd be on the first plane out tomorrow morning.

He was beginning to know his wife, to sense her vulnerabilities; she would think he didn't want to say goodbye and that would hurt her. "Right now."

"But, sir, the telephone lines are down because of the mud slide. There is no other way to call."

He looked at his watch again. Twelve-thirty. If he got through right now, she would be asleep, but he'd damn well have someone wake her up.

She would think he'd done this deliberately. After their argument, the things they'd said to each other, she couldn't believe otherwise.

And the first plane left at dawn. He looked at his watch for the third time. "Let's go," he said to his aide. "If we can't get the damned phones to work, I've got to get back to the capital."

"But, sir, the airports are closed because of the weather."

The weather. *Will you understand, Selena? Will you realize that the "every night at eight" pact is at the mercy of the elements?*

"We'll drive," he told his aide.

"But, sir—"

Saber whirled on the man and froze him with a steely eye. "Look, Marcus, lay out all your objections at once. Spit them out. Because if you say 'but, sir' to me one more time, I am going to fire you. Do you understand?''

The man gulped and nodded.

"Now, get me a car. One with four-wheeled drive. We may have to work our way around some mud, but we're going home. Tonight."

Selena folded her jacket away in the overhead compartment and smoothed her skirt as she sat down in the first-class section of the airplane. She smiled at the flight attendant, who, with some surprise, had welcomed her aboard.

The reporter waiting at the entrance to the airport hadn't been surprised, she thought as she fastened her seat belt. She'd wondered who had informed him about her departure. She'd also had to deal with the man's questions—where was she going, why was she flying commercial, when would she be back—before she could make her way to the plane.

The hatch was sealed; the attendants took seats and buckled themselves in.

Selena laid her head against the seatback and waited for the sound of the engines to rev up in preparation for takeoff. Her eyes closed and immediately an image of Saber appeared behind her lids. The resolute decision she'd made last night to take the first flight out this morning didn't seem like such a good idea at the moment.

He'd known she was leaving. If he'd only called to say goodbye. She didn't want to tell him about the baby over the telephone, but she might have done so, anyway. Would it have made a difference? She would like to think so. She would like to think he'd be thrilled. As thrilled as she was.

Suddenly she sat up, filled with anxiety. What if something had happened to him? Oh, God.

The noise of the engines swelled to fill the cabin. She fumbled with her seat belt. She had to get back to the palace. Now.

The attendant noticed what Selena was doing and shook her head frantically.

"I have to get off," Selena mouthed over the cabin noise. The woman's jaw dropped, but she recovered quickly and reached for the telephone on the wall beside her.

In minutes the roar subsided. Selena felt a surge of relief as the buckle finally popped open. The other passengers were looking at each other. She grabbed her carryon bag and stood.

The flight attendant spoke into her phone again, glanced at Selena, said something else and hung up. She met Selena at the hatch.

"I'm awfully sorry to inconvenience you. Please..." She gestured helplessly to the other people. "I apologize, but it's very important."

The woman looked puzzled but she didn't hesitate. "Yes, ma'am," she said. "You forgot your jacket."

The copilot had come from the flight deck to open the hatch. The other passengers watched with curious interest.

Selena could see the stairs being rolled forward as she took her jacket from the young woman. "Thank you." She looked out into the sunshine, anxiously impatient.

And then all words were stolen from her.

Saber looked grim. His hair was disheveled, his shirt and trousers were rumpled and his tie askew. He took the rolling stairs two at a time; before they even reached the plane he was at the top. She stepped out to join him. "Saber, what on earth—"

He gripped her arm. She could feel the tension in his fingers. "Selena—" He broke off and looked around in frustration. The flight crew stood a scant three feet away. At the bottom of the steps she could see two airport guards, and more reporters. A mud-splattered Range Rover was parked at an angle to the tarmac and Saber's aide waited by the open door.

A strong gust of wind picked up his tie and flung it over his shoulder. "Selena—" he said again.

One of the reporters put his foot on the first step and the move set off a strong resolve in Selena. She shook off the air of bewilderment that had slowed her reflexes.

She put a smile on her lips and turned to the flight crew. "Something has come up that necessitates my postponing my trip." She held out her hand to the pilot. He took it. Without haste she shook hands with the rest of the crew, calling them by name. "Thank you very much for your kindness," she said and smiled at Saber. "Shall we go?"

The reckless gleam in Saber's eye sent her heart up into her throat and almost brought her to a halt, but she met it with a warm smile. He smiled, too. His smile didn't, however, quiet the mounting dread that her husband might deck one of the reporters if any one of them tried to interfere. She disengaged her arm from Saber's grip and switched positions so that her hand was now in the crook of his arm. From there, if he needed it, she could give him a warning pinch.

But they managed to get past the reporters with a noncommittal word or two. At last they reached the Rover. She wondered where the vehicle had come from. It certainly wasn't Saber's normal mode of transportation. It didn't have the tinted windows of his limousine, either, so she and Saber had to maintain polite expressions until they reached the outer perimeter of the airport. But, on the seat between them, he held her hand in a tight grip.

She started to speak, but he stopped her with a warning glance at his aide. She settled back in the seat. It wasn't a long drive to the palace, but they sailed right past the gates.

She turned her head to look back. "Where are we going?" she asked, worried now.

He squeezed her fingers. His smile was strained. "It's a surprise."

A surprise? She lifted a brow. Surprises weren't Saber's forte. What was going on?

At last they pulled off the highway and began to climb a hill. The car stopped in the courtyard of what appeared to be a private residence. He helped her out of the car and took a key from his pocket. "Come back in an hour," he told the aide, and didn't wait for an answer.

He opened the door and turned to look at her. "Come in," he invited.

The entrance hall was dim. Saber flipped on a light and led the way into a living room.

Suddenly she was overwhelmed. The house was completely empty. She swung to face him, a dawning smile illuminating her face. "Saber, is this what I think it is?"

At the sight of her smile, he relaxed a fraction. He draped an arm over her shoulders and guided her to the wall of glass overlooking the sea. "And what are you thinking, wife?"

Her voice dropped to a hopeful whisper. "Is this ours?" she asked, expectant, but unable to believe in the dream until he actually said it was so.

He framed her face with his large hands. "It is ours if you agree. Selena, I've never felt so frustrated in my life as I did last night at eight o'clock. The telephone lines were knocked down by the same mud slide that blocked the main road. And the airport was closed in by fog."

She listened openmouthed, watched his face—so open to her now—with growing wonder, able to feel the frustration he'd felt, able to experience his anxiety. She started to speak.

"No, let me finish. I couldn't talk with you. I had no way to reach you or communicate with you. Or touch you." He did that now, his fingers moving a strand of her hair aside, lingering to caress her cheek. He looked at her, not making any effort to hide his love, to control the emotion or the moisture in his eyes. "I thought it would kill me," he murmured. "I love you, Selena.

"I know that I've seemed detached but I no longer want to be that way. I cannot stand the physical isolation from you, either. I love you more than I thought it was possible to love anyone. I want you, not only in my apartment, or a house, but in my bedroom. And if you don't want that, too, I'll have the driver turn right around and take you back to the airport. I don't mean I'll let you go, because I'll never do that. But you can go to your parents' home. I'll continue to call every night at eight but I'm warning you the first time I hear any weakening in your voice, I'll come to get you immediately."

She raised her hand to his face and let all the love she felt for this difficult man shine through her eyes. "Saber, I love you, too. Our pact to be together every night at eight was symbolic, don't you see? I'm sorry you couldn't get through last night, but I wasn't testing your commitment."

"Then why are you going home? Why are you leaving me?" he demanded harshly.

The harshness was born of grief, she saw. "Because I have an appointment, a special appointment." She smiled so he wouldn't misunderstand. "With a man who specializes in taking care of older pregnant women. But I can wait to leave until tomorrow."

"You're going to have a baby?" he said softly. His eyes narrowed as the knowledge made its impact. He looked suddenly as though he found it hard to breathe.

"Not just me. Us." She grinned. "And I hope you're happy, Nicholas. Because I'm ecstatic."

He began to smile, the worry and the tension melting from his face. The expression of relief brought tears to her own eyes. Finally he folded her in his arms against his broad chest. She could hear his heart racing. He stroked her hair and murmured her name. She snuggled closer and was just getting comfortable, when he raised his head.

He was frowning. "You are going to see a specialist? What's wrong? Are you having problems? Because I'd love a child, Selena, but I won't take a chance with your health."

She spent the next hour reassuring him as they toured their new home. They paused at the front door on their way out.

"I'm not jealous anymore."

What an odd thing to say, thought Nicholas. "Jealous? Of who or what?"

"Of Lisha," Selena admitted. She'd never told him this before. "I was horribly jealous of her at first. Everyone adored her."

He caught her close to his side. "Ah, Selena. You never had a reason to be jealous. Lisha was my wife and I loved her," he said. "But you are my wife now and I love you, because you will always walk beside me, not behind me."

When they finally returned to the palace, Saber was immediately swamped by members of his staff. The questions began as soon as they entered the building.

He gave her an apologetic smile. She stood on tiptoe and kissed his cheek. "See you at eight," she whispered and disentangled her fingers from his grip. Her smile held the promise that tonight, during their private hour, they would not do a lot of talking.

As she mounted the stairs to their apartment, she felt his eyes on her back. She heard him say that the situation at the border had been resolved.

The situation between them had been resolved, as well.

She would be waiting for him tonight at eight o'clock and every night for the rest of their lives.

Epilogue

Saber collapsed into a chair that someone had thoughtfully pushed behind him. "A girl," he said weakly.

"A girl," the beaming nurse confirmed as she lifted his daughter up for his inspection. He held Selena's hand as he'd been holding it for the past six hours. In reality, though, she had sailed through labor with very little help from anyone.

"She's beautiful, isn't she?" said his wife a short while later, her eyes drooping slightly with weariness.

"She's perfect."

A girl, he thought in growing wonder. Like her mother—only beautiful, independent, intelligent. Everything a woman should be.

Saber leaned down to kiss his wife with all the tenderness and love he'd learned from her over the past seven months.

Selena had passed the competency test insisted on by the university, with flying colors. And when classes began last fall, her course in government, focused toward women, had begun, too.

She had been nervous, afraid that no one would sign up. Ever concerned, she'd wanted reassurance that she was, indeed, making a difference in the young democracy. After that week of registration, she never asked for reassurance again.

Her class was mobbed, and the university asked if she would consider teaching full-time. She was still thinking that over. With a new baby and a new house, her days would be full. And her nights were reserved for Saber.

"I'm very proud of both of you," he murmured.

"Saber? I asked you if you still like the idea of naming her for my mother."

He smiled. Turnus would be thrilled. "Yes, I like Janie."

She laughed softly. "You were a million miles away."

"No, just twenty years or so," he mused.

"What were you thinking?"

"What a fine marriage we'll arrange for this one." His grin was devilish. "I already have someone in mind."

He ducked to avoid the flying pillow.

*   *   *   *   *

NORA ROBERTS

Love has a language all its own, and for centuries, flowers have symbolized love's finest expression. Discover the language of flowers—and love—in this romantic collection of 48 favorite books by bestselling author Nora Roberts.

Starting in February, two titles will be available each month at your favorite retail outlet.

In February, look for:

Irish Thoroughbred, Volume #1
The Law Is A Lady, Volume #2

In March, look for:

Irish Rose, Volume #3
Storm Warning, Volume #4

Collect all 48 titles and become fluent in

THE LANGUAGE of LOVE

From the popular author of the bestselling title
DUNCAN'S BRIDE (Intimate Moments #349)
comes the

LINDA HOWARD

COLLECTION

Two exquisite collector's editions that contain four of
Linda Howard's early passionate love stories. To add
these special volumes to your own library, be sure
to look for:

VOLUME ONE: *Midnight Rainbow*
Diamond Bay
(Available in March)

VOLUME TWO: *Heartbreaker*
White Lies
(Available in April)

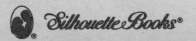

Take 4 bestselling love stories FREE

Plus get a FREE surprise gift!

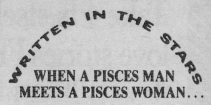